Atchley

Atchley

David Green

STATION HILL ARTS
BARRYTOWN, LTD.

Published under the Station Hill Arts imprint of Barrytown, Ltd., Barrytown, New York, 12507, as a project of The Institute for Publishing Arts, Inc., a not-for-profit, federally tax exempt, educational organization.

Online catalogue and purchasing: http://www.stationhill.org
E-mail: Publishers@stationhill.org

Cover painting, "La Reproduction Interdite" by Rene Magritte, © 1998 C. Herscovici, Brussels / Artists Rights Society (ARS), New York, and with the courtesy of Museum Boijmans Van Beuningen, Rotterdam.

Grateful acknowledgement is due to the National Endowment for the Arts, a Federal Agency in Washington, DC, and to the New York State Council on the Arts for partial financial support of the publishing program of The Institute for Publishing Arts.

Text design and typesetting by Chie Hasegawa
Cover design by Susan Quasha
Backcover photograph of David Green by Maribel Longueira Mira

Library of Congress Cataloging-in-Publication Data

Green, David, 1953-
  Atchley / David Green.
   p. cm.
  ISBN 1-886449-52-X (alk. Paper)
  I. Title.
  PS3557.R3663A94 1998
  813'.54—dc21
                 97-32040
                 CIP

Manufactured in the United States of America.

ACKNOWLEDGMENTS

In the course of writing the present study I have incurred countless debts. The first, and most important of these, is to Michael Fletcher, who allowed me unconditional access to the early drafts of *Landfall*, the letters Atchley wrote to him from Galicia, and the manuscript notes of the *chinoiserie*. Indeed it may be said that had it not been for Mr. Fletcher's generosity and encouragement, this study would never have been undertaken. I am also grateful to him for his illuminating remarks concerning the influence of the unique culture and topography of northwest Spain on Atchley's writing during the years of his residence there. I also want to thank Ray L. Heron, Provost of the University of South Texas and Professor L. N. Coward for graciously relieving me of the burden of employment and allowing me the liberty to devote myself to this project, the Hollis C. Elwood Foundation for the stipend bestowed in conjunction with their Distinguished Scholars Award, and the staff at the Harry Ransom Humanities Research Center in Austin, Texas, for their helpfulness in providing access to the collection of Atchley's letters and manuscripts in their possession.

I extend special thanks to Manuel Salsipuede, who, from the outset of this study, provided crucial help not only with the language of his native Galicia, but also with its folklore and customs; to Linda Weyman for taking the time to help me grasp the Chinese context of Atchley's early work; to Omid Soojodi for his help in preparing the typescript; and to Natasha Synessios for reading and commenting on parts of the text during the initial stages of research. For their comments and moral support I gratefully acknowledge Fernando Alonso, the Ammerman family, Richard and Sheila Bailey, Mary Boon, Maricuela Castroviejo, Beckie Gardiner, Constante González, Julian Honer, José Liste, Angela Llanos, Jill and Stephen

Mindham-Walker, Ellen O'Brien, Manoli Palacios, Susan Primelles, Dr. Augusto Villanueva, the seniors at Mt. Erin, and my family.

Finally I wish to thank the editors of *Theory and Discourse* and *Studies in Ontology* for granting permission to reprint those portions of this study that have appeared in their journals.

PREFACE

The problems posed by an author who questions whether truth can be conveyed without art, and whose express purpose is to undermine the privileged status of critical language cannot be easily dismissed by those who would render a critical interpretation of his or her work. In Atchley's case these problems include willful attempts to mislead the reader in order to break down the conventional boundaries between "truth" and "fiction." His purpose, simply put, is to discredit the metaphysical assumption of an immutable presence underlying all formulations of truth in language, particularly the language of literary criticism. In practice he does this by combining an unpublished theoretical text, "The Art of Absence," with a narrative text, *Landfall*, to create a self-reflexive work that is neither theory nor fiction, but an unstable combination of the two. By blurring his intentions, Atchley is able to question whether there is anything inherent in language that allows us to determine the "real world" validity of its content without resorting to the kind of preferential context he is seeking to challenge. Forced to rely on something as vague as intention or context to determine whether language is present as truth or absent as fiction, we may rightly ask how it is possible to verify or convey the nature of our own presence with any certainty, how language may embody or represent a fixed consciousness distinct from the flux of cultural, psychological, and physiological influences that compete for context at any given time.

Because the challenges of Atchley's writing are both deepened and broadened by a philosophical agenda that requires at least a general understanding of issues addressed in the arguments of contemporary philosophy, we will begin the first chapter of this study with a necessarily brief introduction to the metaphysics of presence. Overall we will follow the order of material as it appears in the composite text. The first half of this book will therefore be devoted to a detailed consideration of "The Art of Absence" and the second to an analysis of the sources, narrative technique, and literary significance of *Landfall*.

Finally I must apologize for not being able to provide the reader with the correct pagination of the published version of Atchley's work. This is due to unforeseen delays in printing. Fortunately, Atchley and his publisher have granted interested parties (with deadlines of their own) permission to cite passages from "The Art of Absence" prior to publication, hence the references to the original pagination of the typescript.

I

Nothing is as central to our understanding of the world, and our conception of ourselves within the world, as the idea of presence. Yet nothing is more elusive. Even to speak of the *idea* of presence may be misleading when centuries of consideration have failed to determine if in fact we are referring to an idea or a predicate, a construct or a feeling. When we reflect on our own presence do we conceive of ourselves as objects or as something independent of ourselves as objects? If as something independent, is that something consciousness or a consciousness of consciousness? Other questions arise when we attempt to distinguish between being present *now*, and presence as an aggregate of moments. If we allow that presence is divisible into a series of present moments we may wonder if our presence *now* is the same thing as our presence *then*, or if we are ever entirely present. Part of the problem is that historically the same word has been used to signify different things. Originally "present" meant "to be before the senses," but when Plato divided existence into the perceptible and the intelligible, he recognized an order beyond what is present, a perfect and enduring Presence that serves as a model for the world of changing moments. And in the process he secured a system of derivative oppositions (eternal and temporal, soul and body) that has been the target of much recent criticism, and may ultimately prove to be the undoing of our search for epistemological certainty.

In the history of metaphysics some form of transcendent Presence was accepted as a first cause or fundamental premise for two thousand years, that is, until Descartes made the point that how we determine presence precedes our knowledge of what is present. Method became more important to our knowledge, and the objects of knowledge increasingly less. What was known became how it was known; what was represented became how it was represented. And the "I think" came before all else as an indisputable proof of individual presence. Kant attempted to stem the tide of empirical skepticism that ensued by asserting the notion of presence on new

1

grounds. His noumenal "thing-in-itself" allowed for existence where there is no empirical certainty. Instead of disintegrating into "a bundle or collection of different perceptions," as Hume would have it, subjective presence was granted new life as a noumenal entity beyond the realm of proof—but at some cost. The centuries since Kant have seen a marked loss of confidence in both the method and language traditionally used to ascertain fundamental truths about what is. Nietzsche would not allow the simple statement "one thinks" to pass without arguing that "one" is "only a supposition, an assertion, and assuredly not an 'immediate certainty.'" Heidegger claimed that the tradition of philosophy has been undermined by its willingness to accept "Being" as self-evident, and, more recently, Derrida has attempted to deconstruct "the authority of presence" by showing how it is an illusion of fixity that ignores the flux of opposition from which it has arisen.

Nowhere are we more present than in the words we recognize as our consciousness, the symbols we use to retain presence and translate personal experience into something approaching the universal. Though we would not exclude our perceptions and impressions from that composite we identify as ourselves, few would argue that our recollection of a summer rain or the neuralgia in a knee constitutes an identity in itself. What is crucial in distinguishing ourselves is the way we reflect, order, and authorize our perceptions in words. Most people accept that the truth about themselves lies in an accurate description of their experiences, their preferences, or their innermost feelings, and not in momentary sensations. We have a natural impulse to seek what is constant and what better way to apprehend and secure a permanent identity out of the flux and chaos of experience than language, the impervious vault that contains the soul of Dante, the spirit of Shakespeare?

If our presence is associated with, or even dependent upon, our words, then an understanding of what we are necessarily involves an understanding of the way these words are present, or are able to convey presence. Is language, for example, inherently present or only determined to be present by our intentions? Or, to take the question a step further, is there anything in language itself that allows us to determine if it is true or false, and if not, is there a satisfactory way of ensuring that it can at least function accurately as a conveyance of presence? According to Atchley, his essay "The Art of Absence" began with just such an inquiry into the relationship between truth and language after he had mistakenly sent a philosophical paper entitled "The Apostasy Brochure" to his publisher instead of a short story he was writing at the time, and his editor had accepted it as fiction without comment.[1] His rigorous attempts at validating an argument through painstaking logic had been read by a highly educated, sympathetic friend as mere invention, the whims of the imagination. Without an explanation external to the text there appeared to be no way to determine whether his writing was fiction or non-fiction. He looked for other examples of mistaken intention and could find very few, but he did notice that the works of many literary authors included documented events from their lives that were widely accepted as fiction when located in their novels or stories. On April 10, 1903 a young Irishman living in Paris received a telegram reading "MOTHER DYING COME HOME FATHER." On June 16, 1904 a young Irish teacher walking along Sandymount Strand recalled a telegram reading "MOTHER DYING COME HOME FATHER." The first telegram was "real" while the second was "fictive." The first referred to the cancer of a forty-four-year-old wife and mother. The second was a passing thought in the consciousness of a fictional character. Atchley accepts the reality of the first telegram because he accepts, without empirical evidence, the accuracy and integrity of Herbert Gorman, who was cited as the source of this information in Richard Ellmann's biography of Joyce.[2] And he accepts the accuracy and integrity of Ellmann on the basis of his international reputation as a Joycean scholar. More often than not, Atchley points out, "our determination of the

---

[1] Atchley's letter to Fletcher dated May 24, 1987.
[2] Richard Ellmann, *James Joyce* (New York: Oxford University Press, 1959), p. 133.

factual content of texts relies on such concatenations of credibility or assumptions based on vague notions of context."[3] What is crucial here is that there is nothing inherent in either telegram to determine whether it is real or not, whether it has presence in the world, or is merely make-believe. The same point may be made about statements whose legitimacy can be assessed without reference to historical fact. Atchley offers the following selections from two well-known writers: "Death is not an event in life: we do not live to experience death. If we take eternity to mean not infinite temporal duration but timelessness, then eternal life belongs to those who live in the present," and "one can understand that the word 'death' should have no meaning for him; situated outside time, why should he fear the future?" Both of these selections appear to mean the same thing: eternity is not associated with longevity but timelessness. The first may be found in Wittgenstein's *Tractatus Logico-Philosophicus* while the second occurs in the final book of Proust's *Remembrance of Things Past*.[4]

The reality or unreality of a text, Atchley concludes, can only be established by its context, which involves the intention of its author. Wittgenstein had meant for his remarks to address concerns of the "real world." Proust had meant for his to contribute to an imaginative depiction of a fictitious character. But what is real and what is fictitious? For the purposes of metaphysics reality is presence, but presence, as we have seen, doesn't always mean what is present. In fact true Presence, the ideal, is never truly present. According to Plato, what is real is precisely what is not before the

---

[3] All references are to the typescript in the possession of MIchael Fletcher, henceforth referred to simply as "Absence." See page 4.

[4] Ludwig Wittgenstein, *Tractatus Logico-Philosophicus*, trans. D. F. Pears and B. F. McGuinness (London: Routledge & Kegan Paul, 1961), p. 72, proposition 6.4311. And Marcel Proust, *Remembrance of Things Past*, trans. C. K. Scott-Moncrieff and Terence Kilmartin, 3 vols. (London: Chatto & Windus, 1981), III, p. 906.

senses, but is instead intelligible to the mind. Logic is therefore real, although it has no empirical presence, no place in the world of the senses. And a flowering dogwood, while existing to the senses, is not real because it is impermanent. In this scheme of things fiction and falsehood would be the absence of Presence, or a present absence. But then so would most things we are familiar with in this world, including our own physical nature.

Atchley believes that the search for ultimate truths in metaphysics has had a profound effect on our attitude toward language. By encouraging an "unholy preference" for the precision of abstraction it has produced a suspicion of everyday experience and the metaphorical or literary language that reflects it. This precision, he argues, achieved by honing word against word, idea against idea, is like the sharpness of a sword that extends beyond its steel. A system of knowledge built on such absurdities can only result in "insensitivity and alienation." It is as important, Atchley maintains, for us to be in touch with the origins of our words as it is for us to be in touch with the sources of our food, shelter, and the various objects that accompany us on our journey through life. True understanding and spiritual integration require our participation in the processes of this world, and metaphor is how we achieve that in language. "We lose our world," he declares, "when we are seduced by the facility of an unconscious or habitual language." The most dubious "achievement" of our species is communication without connection. As Atchley puts it, "We are content with a pantry in the palace, quite satisfied to let unconsidered words escape from unknown places with no experience of their primal beauty and passion, no trace of their passage through time, their survival in fields of famine, their corruption in schools of tedium, and their vivid resurgence in childhood's sacred hollows of discovery."[5]

In order to demonstrate what he means by "an unconscious or habitual language," Atchley examines the distance between the contemporary use of several of the most operative words

---

[5] "Absence," p. 5.

in his essay and what he calls their "ancestral ghosts." While acknowledging that the metamorphosis of meaning does not imply that what is new is somehow inauthentic, he does believe that many of the words we use today are deceptively inappropriate and have lent themselves to concepts "inconsistent with sensory or intellectual experience." He begins by asking what we mean when we speak of "truth" as the ultimate goal of philosophy. Are we alluding to some kind of rational perfection beyond the world in which we live, an eternal model of our world like the one referred to in the *Timaeus*? Is this the same thing we mean when we say that a person speaks the truth? Do we participate in something? Is your truth necessarily the same thing as my truth? "Truth," as that which conforms to fact, has a much shorter history in English than "true," which first meant "steadfast," or "loyal," referring to someone who was unwavering or solid in support. The more speculative etymologies trace "true" back to a source that it shares with "druid," the Sanskrit word *dru*, which means "tree." That philosophy would seek conclusions as solid and unchanging as a tree Atchley finds perfectly reasonable, much more so than the absurdity of absolute perfection or permanence, a concept he attributes more to a psychological need than to anyone's personal experience.

Another word that interests Atchley is "fiction," commonly held to be the opposite of fact. We believe a newspaper report generally to be factual and a novel to be fictitious. The report "re-presents" what actually happened while the novel creates an imaginative experience. The former refers to a "real world" presence and the latter does not. The word "fiction" derives from the Latin *fingere*, which means to fashion or shape a plastic material, something, at any rate, with tangible properties. The word "fact" comes from *facere*, which can also mean to make or fashion something (as in *manufactura*). Though both can denote the activity of making, the former was tainted with the darker connotations of fabrication and invention while the latter was held in higher regard as producing something concrete and real (despite the shadowy similarity between "factitious" and its cousin "fictitious"). This leads Atchley to ask whether language, as something fashioned by human beings, should be considered a figment or a fact. For philosophers and critics it must be a fact, for how could something ephemeral convey something that is eternal? And yet, he asks, haven't we just seen how arbitrary and impermanent are the meanings of words? Truth, he concludes, is not merely conveyed by art, but constituted by the very figments it seeks to dispel.

The distinction between fact and fiction is itself artificial, one more invention of *homo faber*, and reflects a deep-seated conflict in our nature. On the one hand we want something certain, something timeless, to encourage us to believe in the permanence of our being, while on the other we want the freedom to follow our imaginations, to create our destinies without the imposition of logical or physical restraints. Atchley believes that art comes closer to satisfying both of these needs than philosophy (although strictly speaking he believes that philosophy, as the "rhetorical enhancement of fiction," is a kind of art and that the realm of its endeavors is "a wonderful La Mancha"). He appreciates the efforts of Vico to equate the *verum* with the *factum*, the truth with what is made, and goes so far as to claim there are no truths beyond the creations of human culture (which include social custom, language, and the paradigms of thought), and that art provides all the permanence we can bear. Atchley closes the first part of his essay with a brief discussion of the poetry of Shakespeare, Keats, and Yeats where, he says, the words or objects of artistic creation are seen as offering a transcendent, more enduring presence than life itself.

The second part of "The Art of Absence" pursues the argument that the language of literature is not only present as a palpable creation of human enterprise, it is more permanent than our lives which are continually changing and progressing toward a relatively swift termination. The challenge for literature lies therefore not so much in establishing its presence, as in using that presence to represent our transience and ultimately our absence. It has done this by exposing the illusions behind our habitual acceptance of an ontological pivot in a tradition of doubt decidedly older and more irreverent than that of metaphysics. To demonstrate

7

how permanent texts can appear to belie their own stability Atchley examines a selection of works ranging from *The Arabian Nights* to *The Unnamable*. The most any of these works can achieve, however, is an *impression* of ontological fragility through the carefully orchestrated subversion of narrative presence effected most often in an apparent loss of temporal consistency or authorial control. Though the illusion of unpredictability is an integral part of fiction, there is, Atchley reminds us, "no more latitude in the outcome of events than there is in the placement of pieces in a jigsaw puzzle."[6] Those three headstones high up on the slope next to the moor will always mark the same sleepers in that quiet earth. What happens on the printed page happens once and forever. Thus the novel or short story, unlike jazz or impromptu theater, has no means of presenting anything truly in process. Apparent examples to the contrary, such as the blank chapters of *Tristram Shandy* and the autonomous insurgence of Dr. Fileno's dispute with the author in Pirandello's "The Tragedy of a Character," may suggest the attributes of progressive time, but these works "have as little chance of presenting absence or becoming as insects fixed in amber have of flying."[7] What they do achieve, we are told, is an effect similar to that of distorted perspective in visual art: an estrangement from the technical illusions to which we are accustomed.

Having established the paradoxical presence of fiction on the basis of its permanence, Atchley goes on to argue that its

---

[6] In the history of a text an exception to this may occur when uncertainty over the author's intentions, indicated by his or her reworking of material, technical inconsistencies and outright mistakes, or even poor initial editing, allows the proliferation of variant texts. Among the notable attempts to overcome such uncertainty are the endless editorial emendations of Shakespeare's canon, the hypothetical compilation of Proust's *Remembrance of Things Past*, the revised editions of Joyce's *Ulysses*, and, perhaps most surprising of all, the new edition of Coleridge's poetry produced by J. C. C. Mays. It seems fitting that much of Atchley's own writing remains in an unedited state awaiting scholarly interpretation to fix its definitive presence.

[7] "Absence," p. 8

inventiveness, the fact that it creates situations that have not happened in the "real world," should be no impediment to our belief in its capacity to provide knowledge, purpose, and value in our lives, to address the questions we need to ask in a meaningful way. To say that the element of fantasy in literature disqualifies it from the realm of "actual" experience is like saying that people are only real when their thoughts are infallible reflections of a thoroughly knowable world. Do we cease to exist when we daydream or wonder or read a novel? Are we nothing more than a mirror made of flesh and blood? Atchley sees the mind as a self-integrating (and therefore self-creating) combination of words and impressions that may lose or distort its experience according to its needs. He believes that the myth of the mind as some kind of permanent entity comes from the notion that its words and impressions are subject to the scrutiny of "an unchanging witness or managing editor," in other words, that there is an aspect of the mind which reads its contents the way a reader reads a novel and is perfectly stable and consistent even though the thoughts that pass before it may change as radically or as incongruously as a surrealist fantasy. But Atchley argues that this ideal editor who can invariably distinguish "fact" from "fiction" is more a fiction than a fact—not because there is no editor, but rather because this editor is a product of the imagination, which "elevates our greatest needs to transcendent truths." Like a novel, the mind has as many readers as it has occasions of being read. And just as most readers agree on what they are reading most of the time, so too the mind maintains a certain consistency in its interpretation of mental events, but it is not above the distorting influences of prevailing needs.

Despite the obvious differences between thinking and reading, Atchley believes that the lasting mental events created by literature are essentially no different from those created by "real world" experience (whether immediate or secondhand). To illustrate this point he asks us to consider the nature of the images produced by both kinds of phenomena. First he asks us to think about an elderly neighbor from our early childhood. Then, referring to a passage from his Chinese journal, he describes the scene on a road in the eastern suburbs of Wuhan. A man is sitting on a red stool outside a whitewashed building having his hair cut as trucks and cars and motorcycles rush by stirring up clouds of dust. And assume, he says, that you, as the ideal reader of these lines, are familiar with Joyce's character Leopold Bloom. You have an image of Bloom in mind, in fact, a very vivid picture of him eating his cheese sandwich at Davy Byrne's pub. You know as much about him as any other literary character you have ever encountered and probably more than you know about most friends and acquaintances since Joyce provided abundant examples of his character's thought. If a scientist with no knowledge of your acquaintances probes your mind and discovers the images of your neighbor, the roadside barbershop, and Bloom at lunch, would he or she be able to tell which one was "real" and which was not? At this point Atchley reveals that there was no man in Wuhan, that the scene he described is one that he sketched from his imagination. Does this change the image of the man in your mind? Is he suddenly less like your neighbor and more like Bloom, or is the only difference the file in which your fictitious editor has decided to place him?

Since the editor of our consciousness, the author of our lives, is essentially absent, we are whatever reality, in its conventional sense as either a permanent truth or an immediate presence, is not. But this reality, Atchley declares, "is nothing more than the path of least resistance in a mind without imagination."[8] It is the product of a mind that has grown weary at the challenge of departure, that prefers the sanctuary of authority, finds comfort in habit, and is antithetical to the process of discovery. This is the terrible irony of metaphysics: those who would seek the truth must deny the permanence of precedent truths, and proceed with a skepticism so radical that it belies the very promise of their search. For Atchley literature may approximate what he paradoxically refers to as the "higher truth of no truth" because it attempts

---

[8] "Absence," p. 10.

to capture "pure seeking," with no responsibility of finding. And that will remain its challenge, because, as he points out, it is as difficult to present a "perfectly independent" imaginative experience in literature as it is to present our absence.

To be liberated from the metaphysics of presence and escape subordination to the authority of theory, a work of fiction must exist outside the mimetic tradition; it must be willing to violate the interdictions of formulaic thought, technique, and intention; it must flow without a plot, without strategy or the necessity of congruity, and with as few reminders of its presence and permanence as possible, pushing the words to the point of unintelligible transparence. It must speak, Atchley says, "like an oracle, from a source of unmediated experience."[9] He doubts whether it is possible to eliminate an authorial influence from a work altogether, but thinks the effort is worthy in itself and discusses various ways of going about it. One is to present a fictional character as the author of a text, such as Arthur Gordon Pym. Another is to create the impression that a text has been taken over by autonomous characters who decide their own fates, which is what we find in the works of Pirandello, Beckett, and O'Brien. In the end, however, it makes little difference which ploys are used to obscure or confuse the voice of the narrative since we always know that somewhere behind the scene someone is directing the words with the purpose of creating a work of art. For example, Atchley says, the reader cannot know beyond a doubt whether Atchley is the author of his narrative works, or is rather a character in works of fiction by someone else. Perhaps he is a character in a work of fiction by a man named Green or perhaps even Green is such a character. In any case author and character are nothing more than events in the mind of the reader; in fact how they exist in the mind of the reader is more important to who they are than who they

---

[9] In his own opinion Atchley has only come close to an "unmediated experience" of writing once and that was in the closing section of *Landfall*. However, in the following story he creates an analogous situation to that of the absent author. This story was originally included in "The Art of

11

really are, assuming that they really are, as far as the reader is concerned. It is always possible that some unscrupulous scholar has created a writer by the name of Atchley to question the assumptions and strategies of critical theory. There is simply no way to determine, from the words that appear on a page, if a person with the name Atchley does or does not exist. Even a successful search for bibliographical documentation is

---

Absence" as a footnote. The person referred to actually lived in a small village in eastern Tibet. His life was chronicled in a collection of accounts by Sir James Bailey entitled *Curious Tales of the Amdo* (Oxford: Waterfield Press, 1912). Atchley's fictional account follows: [On the evening of Tse-pame's sixth birthday his father climbed the snow-covered paths among the peaks behind their village to seek the benefaction of the spirits that haunt the highest passes. At holy spots along the way he fastened prayer-flags to weathered sticks anchored in cairns of mantra stones and on a windless ledge stopped to rest and watch the soaring hawks disappear and reappear from the still blue lake of the luminous sky.

By nightfall he stood alone on the frozen plain of a glacial valley. Snow leopards came down beneath the moon to break the ice and drink. The mountains around him seemed to cower before the immensity of night while lithe strips of cloud streamed from the ragged points of their highest peaks like fine abrasions cut in deep blue marble. Icicles glistened along the rims of granite shelves and on the upper slopes white stupas held silent vigils to a scattering of stars. For an instant he became transparent.

Weeks later his body was found surfacing, like an archipelago, from a field of snow and blue spring flowers. Tse-pame's mother received the news while she and her son were gathering firewood in the forest near the road to Sok Gompa. She fell ill within days. The boy languished. Late that spring a group of monks came down through the valley to the west of the village. Because he had shown the signs that must end their search, and because she had nothing left, could do nothing more for him, they took her only son. He sat impassively when placed in the saddle of a sturdy yak harnessed in embroidered straps strung with bells. But as they began to move away, he turned to look back through the steaming breath of the lumbering beasts at her wistful figure waving and calling to him from the roof of her house.

The snow was still deep in the high passes. The bells and wind and the hooves on the earth were the only sounds that he heard. At night they slept in the yurts of nomads who regarded them as men blessed with the secrets of immortals. He dreamt of his father singing beneath the snow and of the whiteness of the sky where he lay.

The summer months passed quickly. The cold had returned by the time they arrived at a broad river in a desolate valley. On the shore they were

no guarantee of presence since the scholar may have gone to the trouble of fabricating evidence of a literary life and body of work. Whether Atchley is Atchley or the scholar is Atchley, Atchley says, an author, by any name, is the person we encounter on the page.

Another way to challenge authorial influence is to argue or imply that a work of fiction may have a nominal author, but

---

met and ferried across on the inflated skins of animals. They climbed a slope of powdery loess and brown scree to the broken tower that would be his home. It was isolated high on a pedestal of stone, and in the pale evening light its earthen walls seemed lit with a ghostly red candescence. The ground floor was a chanting hall where banners of silk hung like bunting from wooden pillars and acrid smoke rose from butter lamps of liquid amber. On the walls were musty scrolls and the architraves over the doors were sculpted into rows of demons and gods.

His room was at the top of a series of ladders worn with time and polished by soot. It was a cold chamber of low beams and latticed windows. A collection of squat, smiling idols sat on a shelf to one side. Across the room was a couch covered with plump yellow cushions. He was left to himself by the men who had brought him there, somber men who so abstained from speech and gesture as to appear absent in the specter of their presence. The joss sticks on the altar burned themselves out, and he was eased into sleep by thoughts of his mother's garden in the smoky fragrance of a thousand flowers.

Saffron light filtering through saffron curtains filled the room. He woke early and went from window to window with an urgency of wonder. But the valley, frozen still in the shadows of the mountains, showed no signs of life. A man appeared at the door with hot barleycakes wrapped in rags. Nothing was said and soon he was gone. For the rest of the morning no one else came near. In the afternoon soup and tea and cheese were brought. That night he heard chanting coming from below as fierce winds gathered around the eaves.

Snow fell heavily for several hours before the clouds parted and a full moon shone through. Wolves could be seen moving across the distant moraines. At dawn a small man came trudging barefoot up the snowy paths. It was his master. From that day it became their custom to sit on opposite sides of the room from morning till evening speaking with a respectful economy of phrase. The child learned of the world as appearance only and of people as shadows among shadows. He was told that he himself was but night and its silence waiting for the days of his body and the words of his mind to be exhausted. His faith in things began to falter. He was uncertain how to live, what to think.

that that author has no more presence than the editor of the mind, and that he or she exists only in relation to a text or even a reader. In other words the author is a phenomenon of the text rather than an independent identity that produces texts. Atchley is really saying two things here: first, that the person who does the writing is not a single unified entity, but is rather the provisional amalgam of a changing environment,

---

Fearing the loss of days, he would extend them into night, lying awake as the dust of woodworms drifted down through the darkness. So great was his suspicion of appearances that when he rounded a corner he would turn back quickly to see if what he had seen was still there. But the worst of it was that he could not conceive of a way to keep out the silence without using up his allotment of words. Even thoughts, he soon discovered, were nothing more than words. In fact everything he was seemed to be words. Words and days. He tried humming, but felt it too far outside himself, too much like the singing of birds to be of much use.

Then the idea of escape entered his mind. Perhaps if he could go far enough away and forget what he had learned, his ignorance might preserve him. He made his preparations carefully, putting aside a barleycake a day, saving jars and bottles of water. He planted a cache somewhere up among the rocks, and when the larkspurs began to blossom he knew the time had come.

On a sunny morning of stark colors and deep shadows, he went out under the pretense of exercise and walked until he reached the high escarpments. Hawks soared and vanished into the cold blue sky. He crouched in a dusty corner under a rock and ate one of the mealcakes. It seemed like a good place to rest. He took some comfort from the firmness of the stones and the scent of the juniper. These were things he could be sure of, things as old as the night, he thought. Settling himself on the ground he lay his head on his arm and said a silent prayer to the local deities for protection. But he was soon wondering if someone had missed him. Perhaps someone had even seen him leave. He got up quickly and decided to keep walking until nightfall and then hope to find a house or an encampment of nomads. Soon after leaving the shelter of the rocks and without the slightest warning he found himself face to face with two enormous men in sheepskin coats. The red tassels in their hair told him they were brigands from the east, men who would murder for the smallest gain. They investigated his robe, examined his pockets and fingered his bottles, but finding nothing, let him go, laughing as he stumbled in fear of their dogs.

He reached a pass through the mountains just before sunset. The ground was scarred from the traffic of herdsmen and traders and spotted with the dung of their beasts. High on a rock to the right was the skull of a

14

literary influences, impulses, skills, and so on; and second, that this person only becomes an author by virtue of a text, and then only as understood by those who engage the text. What unifies this person in one relatively small aspect of his or her life, what creates a permanent author out of the impermanence of life, is the unchanging presence of the words. Apart from the *factum* of the text, there is no author, and

---

ram. On the left was a cairn where pilgrims had deposited slates inscribed with the holy words of their masters. Strings of red and yellow and white prayer flags stretching across the narrow passage snapped in the brisk wind. At the end of this corridor, where the path dropped away, he stopped and looked out at the snow-covered peaks of the next range. Beneath them, deep among the encroaching shadows of the dusk, lay a vast lake reflecting the clear, colorless sky. He had never seen anything like it, anything so open to his imagination, so suggestive of the entrance to another world. The descent was steep and uneven, the surface mostly gravel, but he hurried down, sliding here and there, excited by his discovery, worried by the night. Several hours later he walked into the compound of a small flat-roofed house and after some questioning was given a place to sleep on the floor in the center of the main room.

He did not waken until well into the next day when he felt his hands being tied with leather cords. The two brigands were quick with their work and soon had him on his feet and out the door of the house. He was taken back up the slope, through the pass, and down the other side, where, once they were within sight of the tower, his ligatures were loosened. Ignoring the blood on his wrists, the monks were satisfied and liberal in their bounty.

Now there would be no more exercise, no more freedom to move. He was housed in a stone hut on a cliff-face accessible only by ladder. It was not, as it appeared, a merely punitive measure. He had been born the mouthpiece of a god. His education had come to an end, and henceforth he would learn from the silence.

It was a silence strictly enforced. Seasons passed. Then years. Not once did he leave his cell. Food and water were hoisted up in a basket on a rope. And twice a year on special occasions he could not name, let alone account for, a group of monks placed the ladder to the cliff and paid him a visit. He was helped into a ceremonial robe of silk and seated on a pile of cushions. The windows were shuttered, incense was lit, and two members of the entourage struck a rhythm on a gong and drum. He was given a potion of aconite, which he drank with calm foreboding, and moments later his body succumbed to a ravaging visitation. His eyes moved wildly, his face dripped with perspiration, and his lips were coated with a white paste. The monks retreated to the corners of the room and watched him

15

ironically, the succession of selves who are unified in the text become as diverse as the various readers who conceive of the author in their own unique ways.

Ever fascinated by the potential of a text to mean more than it says, our interpretations insidiously seek to acquire the rights to its author, to make the author satisfy the needs we have discovered within ourselves through the text. We

---

as his skin blanched and his muscles began to quiver. Slowly at first, and then with gathering speed he turned, tortuously, bending and writhing, spinning, more and more erratically, as if unhinged from the axis of his body, until his collapse was inevitable and he was caught by two young monks who carried him over to the cushions where he was held in an upright position as questions were put to him and his answers carefully recorded. When no more words were forthcoming he was left in the company of a single attendant.

His words were taken back to the tower, copied out on long thin sheets, and added to the records of former scribes bound together under wooden covers. Each response was rigorously studied in light of the vital question that had drawn it from its source. But the words were not all that clear, referring as they did to vague sensual impressions, visions of distant places and the features of people long since transformed by time. Hawks vanishing into the sky at the bottom of a valley, bells beneath the snow, blood streaming through a man's hair were some of the messages misconstrued and further distorted by their application to subjects far beyond the bounds of their relevance.

After each visitation he felt he had lost that much more of himself. In the long hours of his isolation he would cull every corner of his mind for the words to tell himself the story of himself, only to find that they had disappeared. Sometimes he would see an image like that of a lake, but being unaware of a way to articulate the scene or the sense of what he saw, he would wonder if it was not in fact something he had dreamed, something of a former wish or fear. And buried deeply beneath what he wanted to believe was the suspicion that there was someone else, something else, who could know him well enough to plunder his life and live it or tell it in another place, at another time. Plunder until the last corner had been picked clean.

The day came when his thoughts, though they continued to come, came to nothing. Words were there, but on their own. Just the words, the few of them that remained, on their own, coming together by force of habit. And sometimes they managed. And sometimes they didn't. Not that it mattered. That they came but came to nowhere, did not come to him, was nothing to him because he was not there. And the patterns of their coming, circling flights in an empty sky, was the pattern of another's

16

want the images and feelings we experience while reading to become part of the permanence of the *factum*, in a sense we want who we are to share in the immortality of what we read. By making the author more than the words, we "create a transcendent ideal in our own image and likeness." Atchley sympathizes with this need for presence, but points out that the words themselves are as indifferent as the stars in the sky to what we need. "The magnetism of ontology" he says, "is nothing more than fear gathered into Greek, and the being behind the words is as insubstantial as the memories of love that are buried with our mortal bodies."[10] By countering the assumption of an author's presence with the case for his or her absence we can, to a great extent, free a text from the constraints of intention, and participate in the idyll of experience without mediation.

Once we accept that Presence as a first premise is the fiction behind all truths we may begin to reassess the value of human creation, the *fingere* as much as the *facere*, and recognize the artifice in all language-based experience, and, ultimately, in our deluded search for an absolute. Atchley believes that a failure to do this will result in the exacerbation of a kind

---

coming, another's knowing, another's waiting. Or was it the other gone and he remained? Either way it spelled the end. And yet emanating, still emanating, like a spring among the rocks, was a voice among the bones, a surprise to no one in this place to hear the words when there was nothing left alive, when what was left, the nothing left, had been abandoned. Only now the words were unrecorded, heard but unrecorded, as limbs were gathered among folds of wool and taken out to a tablerock high above where hawks float silently in an empty sky, and there the flesh was cut away, the tongue cut out, the heart cut to pieces, the bones at last beaten into silence, mixed with barley-flour and left to the appetite of the sky, drawing from flight by force of habit what would come until the last corner among the rocks had been picked clean of any trace.

It was snowing again when the monks set off to seek the signs that would end their search. A boy was found, as had been prophesied, living beside a lake at the bottom of a valley, where an old legend had it hawks would dive and disappear.]

[10] "Absence," p. 17.

of cultural schizophrenia produced by the conflict between our dependence on a faith in permanence and the obvious temporality of our participation in the world. By confronting and resolving this conflict we may rid ourselves of such metaphysical absurdities as an absent Presence and such moral absurdities as the pursuit of spiritual well-being and immortality through unbridled materialism. To those who would decry such a move as opening the door to moral relativism Atchley points out that all cultural phenomena, including the notions we have of ourselves, are the creations of our minds and have always existed in a state of change. By admitting as much we can relieve ourselves of the suffering brought about by our appetite for perfection, for absolute knowledge, and the false security of an eternal presence.

II

Landfall is a novel unique among the works of Atchley, indeed, among works of contemporary fiction, for having experienced two distinct incarnations, each with its attendant collection of criticism. The first may be dated from 1988 when a limited edition was published in Britain and America. The small amount of critical opinion generated at that time was sharply divided over the question of whether the book deserved publication "as an original work of unparalleled honesty,"[1] or dismissed altogether as an undisciplined and self-indulgent experiment "feeding off the aura of an established author."[2] For several years the text languished as a curiosity, existing almost as an accessory to the critical debate, until Atchley decided to combine the novel with his essay "The Art of Absence" to create a composite text that blurs the traditional distinctions between fiction and non-fiction. *Landfall* was no longer simply a modern allegory describing "a search for spiritual sustenance in a desert of lost faith,"[3] and "The Art of Absence" was no longer simply an essay applying the arguments of neo-pragmatism and hermeneutics to a discussion of fiction. Both works were transformed by their relationship to each other and critical opinion has had to reassess both on entirely new grounds.

A study of the composite work is therefore a study of the *progression* of the author's intentions, that is, how his original strategies in each text were re-defined and continue to be affected by the strategies of its companion piece and the work as a whole. In an interview given a year before the *Landfall* typescript was first mentioned, Atchley described his only recent

---

[1] K. Haney, "Atchley's *Landfall*," *Bedford Review* Jan. 1989: 62.

[2] C. M. L. Bernal, "The Emperor's Clothes," *University Review* XXI (1989): 114-15.

[3] Eldridge MacKenzie, "The Critical Complement," *The New England Review of Books* 2 Feb. 1990: 24.

effort as "a failed attempt to write autobiography."[4] It must have been during this time or shortly afterwards that he began to research the role of the desert in literature, which resulted in an essay on selected works by Beckett, Bowles, Shepard, and Fugard, "Asceticism and Self-Knowledge in Contemporary Literature."[5] The move from autobiography to a critical essay involving philosophical issues more than likely had some bearing on the formulation of the novel and may offer insights into Atchley's interests or even intentions at the time. In the essay he describes the desert as a place "at some remove from the insulating distractions of society, where creative self-reflection once produced the great monotheistic religions of the world."[6] In *Landfall* his protagonist inhabits a world where the beliefs and truths created and enforced by traditional social environments have disappeared, and the isolation of this individual makes him more conscious of the ontological need to create a presence, through language or art, to fill the void. From our knowledge of the genesis and composition of *Landfall* it appears to have undergone a series of metamorphoses from the author's initial effort to capture his presence in biography, to a consideration of the nature of what he was trying to capture, to an inquiry into the question of whether such a thing even exists, and finally to a search for what might take its place.

The effects on *Landfall* of the subsequent addition of "The Art of Absence" were numerous. Most obviously the essay created a theoretical framework for understanding the author's intentions in the novel. Less obviously the combination forced a reassessment of the strict separation of fiction and critical discourse by offering equal credibility to each kind of writing without defining the genre of the work as a whole.

---

[4] Mason Downing, "Presenting the Absent: An Interview with Atchley," *Agnosy* VII (1985): 19-23.

[5] Scheduled for publication in the winter of 1999 in a collection edited by Francis Lucas.

[6] Ibid.

Did *Landfall* become more authentic by appearing in a work of critical theory, or did "The Art of Absence" become less authentic by appearing in a work of fiction? Having succeeded in describing his personal experiences more effectively in allegory than biography, Atchley sought a means of illustrating the reason for this without resorting to the kind of direct, explanatory strategies that had proven insufficient in the first place. By juxtaposing the figurative description of his life in Galicia with a theoretical essay that argues against the hierarchical ascendancy of theory over fiction, he was able to create a vacuum of generic intentionality, or a "non-site" in deconstructive terms, where this reason could emerge from the works themselves. This does not mean that Atchley rejects the value of theory. He apparently spent as much time on "The Art of Absence" as he did on *Landfall*. But it does attempt to show that honest critical expression has no more claim to authenticity than fiction.

The "truth" of what is written in discourse is always determined by an author's rhetorical strengths or weaknesses. In other words, why an author chooses to say one thing and not another depends on his or her ability to use language. There is no "truth" waiting somewhere to be apprehended by the precise words needed to apprehend it; there are only constructions, like sculptures, created out of the materials, skills, and interests available to the author. Our beliefs are therefore not so much what is communicated as how it is communicated, and our intellectual discoveries are no more substantial than the magic of language. Figurative language, unlike "factual" language, allows the reader to participate *openly* in the creation of meaning. It is, as Davidson has said of metaphor, "the dreamwork of language, and like all dreamwork, its interpretation reflects as much on the interpreter as on the originator."[7] For Atchley, communication that allows for creative interpretation cannot claim a truth that is uniformly understood, and for this reason it comes closer to

---

[7] Donald Davidson, *Inquiries into Truth and Interpretation* (Oxford: Clarendon Press, 1984), p. 245.

representing the indeterminate nature of things than factual discourse, which becomes brittle in its efforts to achieve perfect intelligibility. The abundance of metaphorical language and description in *Landfall* and the dearth of argument, even that embodied in a plot, encourages the reader to experience a poetic re-creation of the world that can open the imagination to a rare transparence and even the possibility of absence.

Among the earliest and most perceptive commentaries written on this novel is "La geografía del espiritu," Manuel Salsipuede's study of Atchley's use of the ancient pilgrimage route associated with the shrine of Compostela in his quest for personal renewal.[8] According to Salsipuede this route came into being sometime during the mists of prehistory, perhaps as early as 3000 B.C. judging by the petroglyphs found on granite boulders along the way. Its pre-Christian artifacts and legends, however, are largely associated with the Celtic people, who believed that off the western coast of the known world, where the sun descends into the sea, were the enchanted isles of paradise, a land of eternal youth and happiness. The journey to the end of the world during their lives assured the Celts that their souls would fly directly to paradise after death. And so for thousands of years pilgrims from all over Europe followed the stars of the milky way, or *via lactea*, across the mountains and plains of northern Spain to Cape Finisterre. That is until the ninth century when a hermit living near a Roman necropolis forty miles inland from Finisterre heard celestial music and saw lights in the sky over a particular sepulcher. The local bishop decided that this was a miracle indicating the presence of the tomb of St. James, and the Catholic Church hastily Christianized the pagan route, leaving the last forty miles to those diminishing few whose Christian beliefs maintained vestiges of their pagan past.

It is Salsipuede's contention that *Landfall* is a carefully

---

[8] Manuel Salsipuede, "La geografía del espiritu," *Loureiro* XVI (1990): 3-22.

crafted and symbolically rendered account of Atchley's sojourn in Galicia and that the inward and outward trajectories of the protagonist in the novel are meant to represent the differing philosophical perspectives held by the author upon his arrival in and departure from Santiago de Compostela. To support this thesis Salsipuede argues that Atchley's self-imposed exile followed a period of disillusionment when he became convinced that the fundamental problem in contemporary life is a loss of faith in any unifying presence or purpose transcending the individual:

> Morally he had begun to see what he described as the "skull beneath the flesh" in human behavior, the sublimated brutality of a single-minded instinct for personal gain. Philosophically he no longer accepted the idea of a positive presence or intelligence in the world, and believed that chaos toying with order is the closest thing to divinity we are likely to know.[9]

Salsipuede asserts that the Pyrrhonian strain in much of Atchley's writing through the eighties reflected his growing frustration with the failure of rational attempts to re-establish value in our lives. Essentially he believed that reason had yielded nothing better than a choice between a deluded sense of ontological security and the abyss of moral relativism. When no remedy could be found to satisfy his intellect Atchley discovered what Salsipuede calls "the healing power of the purely experiential."

The desolate landscape of crippled and dying souls, the empty farms, the crumbling tannery, and the abandoned abbey of the first half of *Landfall* are all meant to suggest the passing of a way of life premised on a faith in some higher presence or purpose. It is no coincidence, Salsipuede maintains, that the physical characteristics of this place resemble

---

[9] Salsipuede, "geografia," p. 16 (translated by the author).

those of Galicia.[10] And the narrator's encounter with a vanishing people, whose language and customs reflect a spiritual, often imaginative, view of the world is very likely a veiled depiction of his own experience among the Galician *campesinos* whose legends and tales are known throughout the Spanish-speaking world. The allegorical or even surreal emptiness of the rural journey inland is meant to be contrasted with the excessive fullness of life in the second half of the story, where the narrator learns to overcome his tenacious awareness of his own presence in order to experience the wonder and richness of the world around him. Salsipuede believes this progress from a search for presence amidst absence in the first half of the narrative to an acceptance of absence in the midst of plenty in the second indicates a crucial shift in Atchley's personal philosophy. He is not only recognizing the futility of any institutional or systematic guarantee of presence, he is offering a more practical and ultimately satisfying way of living one's life. Given the appearance of "The Art of Absence" in conjunction with *Landfall*, Salsipuede's account of Atchley's intentions in the narrative now seems remarkably prescient.

---

[10] See also Salsipuede's "Atchley: Pelengrín a Fisterra," *Hoxe* 12 (1993): 11-26, where he has traced the return journey of the second half of *Landfall* from the Roman bridge at Trasouto up over the rising countryside to the moorlands near the village of Hospital, an ancient resting place for pilgrims (included in this segment is the festival at Corpiño, relocated from its actual site forty miles southeast of Santiago). The ring-fort and petroglyphs may be found just above the Fragoso River and the spring from which the narrator drinks is either at the Hermitage of Our Lady of the Snows, or that of St. Peter the Martyr (attending the gate of heaven— this is the first point from which Finisterre, or "Fisterra" in Galician, may be seen). But rather than continue on to Prado de Paraiso (Field of Paradise), Atchley's character appears several miles to the south where he climbs Mt. Peñafiel, site of the Latin inscription, and the central peak of the Pindo massif, La Moa. From there he descends to the abandoned village of San Cibrán, the first of two villages where Atchley rented a house. The large house described at this point in the narrative is now in ruins. The final stage of the journey takes the narrator to the beach just below the village of Curra, where Atchley rented a second house before returning to America.

Avery Matherson, however, makes a good case for an alternative reading of the story in his article "Atchley and the Sempiternal Cycles of Renewal."[11] Seeking to place *Landfall* in the context of a tradition, he argues that the novel reflects a Romantic preoccupation with the conflict between change and permanence. According to this view, the narrator's awareness of his impermanence causes him to see the world as empty, but as he learns to appreciate the diversity and beauty brought about by change he comes to accept the world on its own terms, and even to take pleasure in the things that will outlast him. Matherson believes the hiatus at the center of the novel is crucial for it provides the distancing necessary for a reappraisal of the initial experience. The narrator, like the speaker in "Tintern Abbey," has felt a profound loss, but in his acceptance of the temporality of things, he gains a mature satisfaction that affords the kind of compensation Wordsworth alludes to in his poem. Matherson also finds strong thematic affinities between *Landfall* and Eliot's poem *The Waste Land.* In both works a moral value is bestowed on change because it allows the possibility of spiritual renewal. Matherson draws an explicit parallel between the sterility that results from an unhealthy desire for permanence in the first half of the novel and the emotional and spiritual demise of western culture caused by an inability to change in Eliot's poem. For both writers fertility is only guaranteed through a cycle of birth and death, and the individual must recognize his or her subordination to a larger purpose. This interpretation, in keeping with the Platonism of Wordsworth and the Christian element in Eliot's poetry, concludes with the assertion that the island the narrator seeks at the end of the story (and from which he came at the beginning) is the Platonic realm of souls before birth and after death, and is therefore not indicative of absence, but rather an acceptance of a presence that transcends sublunar experience. Matherson bases this

---

[11] Avery Matherson, "Atchley and the Sempiternal Cycles of Renewal," *Romantic Literature* Winter-Spring 1990: 56-79.

argument on the ancient association of the *via lactea* with the myth of the blessed isles, the dwelling place of departed souls.

Gail E. Maicias, a leading proponent of deconstructionist methods in critical discourse, argues that *Landfall*, on its own and in conjunction with "The Art of Absence," offers a literary non-site or alterity from which philosophy may be investigated without implicitly endorsing its assumptions through the bias of philosophical language. In the first of her two articles on Atchley, "Signing the Non-Site Fiction,"[12] she attempts to show that the two halves of *Landfall* constitute a fictive deconstruction of selfhood modeled on Jacques Derrida's technique of inverting hierarchical priorities. Typically we conceive of ourselves as a presence and relegate absence to what is "other." The project of deconstruction is to create "non-concepts" that can be ascribed to neither of the oppositional terms from which they appear such as presence and absence, speech and writing, or soul and body. This forces a conceptual or linguistic reassessment of the hierarchies inherent in these contraries, and a recognition of the historical contingency of "reality." Maicias contends that by privileging absence over presence in the first half of *Landfall* Atchley undermines the assumption that absence is merely a lack of presence. Nor does he leave the novel with this simple inversion of a conventional hierarchy, for in the second half of the story he emphasizes presence over absence and finally closes with the ontological fate of the protagonist forever undecided. This indefinite suspension of the protagonist's fate Maicias interprets as a fictional representation of the Derridean "trace," which, as she puts it, "sustains a conceptual instability that demands a reconstituted way of thinking."

---

[12] Gail E. Maicias, "Signing the Non-Site Fiction," *Theory and Discourse* June 1992: 1-27. Ms. Maicias is best known for having developed a concept of identity based on a binary code of absence (0) and presence (1) where the characteristics unique to an individual may be configured in a such a way as to constitute an absence-presence "fingerprint."

By using the extreme privation of the desert, the isolation of the individual from the blinding comforts of society and technology, to reveal the essential absence of human existence, Atchley appears to be aligning himself with several of the writers discussed in his essay "Asceticism and Self-Knowledge in Contemporary Literature." Maicias is most intrigued by the parallel between *Landfall* and Beckett's novel *Molloy*. The latter she characterizes as a prototypical example of the deconstructive text where self-knowledge is achieved through an inversion of the presence-absence hierarchy. The first half of the book she describes as illustrating the threat of absence in the temporal process of becoming. The peripatetic Molloy wanders seeking a home where he may establish his presence but only succeeds in continuing on his course until, rootless, anchorless, and without a fixed identity, he declines and gradually merges with the earth. The second half of the book describes a proud burgher sustained by his material identity who is required to leave his home, religion, and community to seek the wanderer. In the course of his quest he achieves self-knowledge, but only after he too has been stripped of the talismans of presence and forced to relinquish his ontological security. At the end of *Molloy* it is unclear whether the substantial citizen, Jacques Moran, has indeed become Molloy, the wanderer, or whether the return to his dilapidated home and continued social exile is meant to indicate he is both and neither. This ambiguity, Maicias asserts, is similar to the uncertain fate of Atchley's protagonist at the conclusion of *Landfall.* In both novels the protagonists of the second half are exiled from the secure comfort of domestic illusions and come to resemble their itinerant predecessors. Absence is therefore the given to which presence is introduced with neither achieving absolute ascendancy over the other.

Unlike a number of other critics, whose interpretations of *Landfall* have been undermined by the combination of the novel and "The Art of Absence," Maicias has viewed this combination as an opportunity to solidify and expand upon her earlier analysis. In her recent article "Atchley's Response to the

Hegemony of Theory in a Postmodern Culture"[13] she argues that in his latest work he has enhanced his deconstruction of the ontological prioritization of presence over absence by proceeding to the application of this method to the contemporary preference for the "truths" of theory over the "fictions" of literature. Although Atchley has placed theory before fiction in the ordering of his book, Maicias claims he has done so only to establish the argument that he is illustrating in the text on the whole, that critical theory is inherently no more valid than fiction since it is subject to individual limitations, intentions, and interpretations and is constituted by the same words and often the same devices and strategies that figure prominently in literary texts. When Atchley introduces an obvious fiction into his critical argument he is, ironically, subverting that argument to demonstrate its validity. If theory is to fiction what presence is to absence, as Maicias seems to be saying by comparing the deconstructive value of the inversion of the presence-absence hierarchy to the inversion of the theory-fiction hierarchy, then those who attempt to deconstruct the presence-absence hierarchy in metaphysics would have to admit to the fictionalization of their own theory, which is precisely, according to this argument, what Atchley does. Maicias acknowledges this critical quandary and confesses that while she would like to be "right" in her argument concerning her interpretation of Atchley's work, she knows that if she is to agree with him, she too must admit that her interpretation is a kind of fiction.

This limited selection of perspectives on Atchley's recent work belies the diversity of critical writing that exists and suggests the potential of that to come. To the biographical, Romantic, and deconstructive approaches we have reviewed here, responses of equal merit from the Freudian, Marxist, and phenomenological schools could be added, if permitted

---

[13] Gail E. Maicias, "Atchley's Response to the Hegemony of Theory in Postmodern Culture," *Deconstructive Theory* 8 (1998): 34-55.

by the scope of the present study.[14] One article that deserves special mention, however, is Edna C. Ohm's "At Play in a Garden of Tropes,"[15] which investigates the fictional nature of all critical activity and analyzes the narrative quality of Atchley's theoretical prose with particular emphasis on the tropological devices, illustrations, delayed revelations, and foreshadowing he has consciously employed to demonstrate that critical writing is essentially quite similar to fiction. What most of these studies have in common is a recognition of the value to both literature and metaphysics of investigating the historical division between "truth" and "fiction." Like all rigid oppositions in our system of beliefs, this one has produced an unhealthy conflict leading to unnecessary illusions and subsequent disenchantment. By portraying the world as a post-holocaust or post-Nietzschean desert of spiritual emptiness Atchley has shown us the need to renew ourselves. By offering a version of the world reconstructed on the basis of human activity, that is, through an honest acceptance of our incalculably complex and ever-changing nature, rather than on the basis of permanent truths, he is shifting the emphasis back towards temporality and contingency, the banished heirs of our Greek fathers.

---

[14] See Melvin Q. Eisner, "A Psychoanalyst Looks at *Landfall*," *Texas Journal of Psychoanalytic Studies* XXXIII (1991): 117-139; Carlos O'Shaughnessy, "Atchley's Dystopic Vision: Hegel's *Aufhebung* Revisited," *Praxis und Ästhetik* Winter (1992): 45-65; Marie St. John Lyzeckski, "A Phenomenological Analysis of Atchley's Failed Intentionality," *Idea, Culture, and Theory* 11 (1995): 34-47.

[15] Edna C. Ohm, "At Play in a Garden of Tropes," *Kerlarap* Winter (1996): 17-27.

III

From Atchley's letter to Fletcher dated February 10, 1998:

Thanks for sending the article on "Absence" from *Studies in Ontology*. I regret now having prepared the manuscript for publication. I had left it unpublished for so long because I felt it was unpublishable. The author's attempts to make sense of it have only reminded me of my initial reservations regarding its shortcomings. While many of the ideas I developed in the essay still seem valid, I feel they could have benefited from more careful articulation. To tell you the truth, I am surprised to discover that a work so opposed to the relevance of critical theory should find itself so vigorously embraced by it. The weakness of the piece lies not so much in its inevitable inconsistencies and imprecision, but in its apparent inability to communicate the ironies I had meant to convey. I know the difference between fact and fiction. If I am ever afflicted with appendicitis be assured I will seek a physician who is also aware of the distinction, and not a metaphysician who will try to explain it. I prefer to think of truth as the Chinese philosopher Chi-Tsang did, divided into the worldly *laukikasatya* and the absolute *paramarthasatya*, the temporal and the void.

The only real delight I have taken from reading *Landfall* again is the memory of the time when it was written. We had rented a farmhouse from friends in a small village called San Cibrán at the foot of Mt. Pindo, an imposing massif of pink granite. From the upstairs floor we could look out over the tops of the orange and lemon trees and see the surf crashing on the distant beach of Carnota. These friends were marionette makers who had gone to India for instruction in that culture's history of the craft. We found ourselves sharing our days and nights with patches of motley, ceramic hands and feet, and brightly painted faces awaiting assemblage and life as they lay strewn on table tops or hanging from the rafters on thin black cords.

The original intention of *Landfall* was not autobiography per se. This is a notion that first appeared in an article written by Salsipuede. Rather, the text began as a "search for presence." But I knew, even before I had finished the first few pages, that I no longer believed in such a thing and wouldn't know the first thing about expressing it if I did. I wouldn't read any more into it than that. Professor Green is right in asserting that I took Bailey's book on the Amdo as my starting point when writing the story "Captive" (he appears to have overlooked the title as well as the Orphic connotations), but any close reading of the original story will reveal to what extent my version is fictional.

All the best,
Atchley

P. S. And, by the way, *Landfall* is not a diary of my time in Galicia, and I am not its narrator. It's a *novel.* While many scenes may be identified with Galicia, many may not. Anyone familiar with the landscape and climate can tell you that. I particularly resent the idea that I was somehow presenting myself in the book.

After receiving a copy of this letter, I became increasingly frustrated with the entire project on Atchley. What was there to say that might not be refuted by the author? Would some letter appear years after our deaths that would contradict everything I might write? One cannot assume that an author is always the best critic of his or her work, but what makes an independent commentator an authority? The sheer force of argument? Who is to know if I am mistaken or not? Certainly Atchley's letter is a blow to my authority, but perhaps his intention is to be evasive, to dislocate any attempt to determine the purpose and meaning of his works. Perhaps I have been seeking the fixed and determined presence of an author's text only to discover that that author has been pursuing the fixed and determined presence of my own text with the intention of subverting it, of demonstrating that his text cannot be apprehended, that it has no presence. Am I a pawn in some kind of demonstration? But given what he has written in "The Art of Absence" wouldn't he have to agree that the truth of his text must lie somewhere in the indeterminate midst of the revolutions created by the pursuits of author and reader?

If he argues that I am wrong in my assertions regarding his work, then he must admit to intentions other than those I ascribe to him. He therefore concedes some authority in his writing, some voice that is indeed a presence. And though he has contended that he was attempting to demonstrate the circularity of intention and therefore the inevitable elusiveness of presence by writing a work that criticizes itself, my statements concerning his work have provoked a stabilizing effect to produce definition and intention. My presence has in a sense guaranteed his. It is incumbent on the literary commentator to respect the wishes of an author, but not to . . .

Because he incorporated criticism of his text into his text, some critics have felt that he was attempting to preclude or even proscribe an independent perspective on his writing, or at least intimidate independent voices by making the fiction and the authority on that fiction indistinguishable. It would be as if *Ulysses* were not only the account of a day in the life of Leopold Bloom, but also an account of Joyce's views on the novel.

[It is as if the author wanted to be his subject, and so there is an imaginative identification with the work as well as the life of the subject, the author of that work. Unable to tell if *Landfall*, for example, is the experience of the author or the subject as author.]

[Not able to distinguish between himself and the text. So there is a kind of "trace" where reader and writer are interchanged in a . . .]

March 1
Arrived at Gatwick early a.m. for conference on the role of literature in a post-ontological culture. Flight was fine except for the obese woman sitting next to me who spilled my drink twice. Had never seen pretzels before. Light rain but afternoon was sunny. Am staying in Belsize Park at the moment. It's easy to catch the train at South Hampstead and go right down to Euston. One leaves every twenty minutes.

South Hampstead	Euston
9:03	9:10
9:23	9:30
9:45	9:50
10:03	10:10

March 3
Ran into Atchley, of all people, outside the main entrance of the college on Malet Street. It was as if I had always known him. He looks just like his photographs except for his hair, which has turned gray. Medium height. Tortoise-shell glasses. He was standing in a group of people and I felt a little awkward introducing myself, but he was very accessible. I said I admired his work. He thanked me and asked me where I was teaching. I explained that I'm currently working on a project. I'm not sure if he heard me correctly as he then said he "understood the difficulties of my profession, and felt no antipathy."?! Humor?

March 4
It's a wonder knower and known didn't somehow cancel each other out. On reflection I felt a little uncomfortable with the encounter because it reminded me of the symbiotic necessity of our relationship, how neither the scholar nor the author is ever entirely independent. It always seems to come back to the question of validity. Is what I am doing valid without someone

34

else's confirmation? Can there be any point to my words without interpretation or acceptance?

When we consider the question of presence in a literary work we must recognize that the presence of words on a page is nothing more than an irregular sequence of inkmarks on paper. Any other presence is purely a phenomenon of the individual imagination, the presence of the reader. For example, when Atchley writes "a clemency of blue" the reader has the freedom to be anywhere in the blueness of life: sitting against a white wall beneath a trellis of red roses overlooking the sea, or in a field of prairie flowers beneath a prairie sky. But is the imagination a presence or an activity? How do we distinguish between what Ricoeur calls agent and action, or Yeats's dancer and dance? How, for example, do we distinguish between the places of love and the act of love? And are the places of love identical to the objects of love, or is the body, even the spirit, merely a means to a higher state of imagination, a place distinct from any presence?

The words of a literary work allow us to create a place distinct from any presence. For example, Atchley's phrase "a clemency of blue" allows the reader the freedom to be anywhere in the blueness of life: beneath a white wall and trellis of red roses overlooking the sea, or in a field of prairie flowers beneath a prairie sky. Black ink on white paper is our only means to cold lithic incursions of mottled granite or fair yellow flowers of gorse blooming like a billion suns reflecting off a sea of green. And out there, beneath the lazy blue of summer lies the Atlantic, as indifferent as a mind deep within a blue of its own.

bluish-white houses high up on the arid slopes of the Rif Mountains, like living in caverns of ice

March 10
Received this in the mail today from Fletcher:
"I don't think I am betraying Atchley's trust in sending you the following. In fact I have the feeling that he wants me to communicate his sentiments to you. I wouldn't take it too personally. Artistic temperament and all that. He's sort of crotchety with everybody."

3 March 1998

Fletcher,

Met this fellow Green at Birkbeck. Don't quite know what to make of him. I couldn't help wondering why my work would appeal to someone like him. We obviously have very little in common. I avoided his lecture, which had something to do with *Landfall.* I was afraid that had I gone, I would have found myself in the position of confirming his assertions through silence or confounding them with condolence.

Best wishes,
Atchley

My work has grown stale to me. The greatest gift is to be able to re-create the world through one's words, to appreciate all its colors, dark and bright. And yet I take the colors and make them dull, digging into the ground beneath the gardens and pavilions to find what soil and rock supports the color, supports the beauty, as if the cold dark earth could explain the iridescence of the iris. Why do I make this effort to explore another's world and not my own, to establish my presence as the elaboration of another's?

March 20

It is all a quest for presence, to be in one's own words, the words, which more than anything else are who we are, the bits and pieces that outlast us when the prison of our being falters and fades. Yet duplicated, replicated, re-created in the imaginations of others, they are nothing more than the shadow of our presence, "modified in the guts of the living." No, the words betray us before they are out, enduring only because they are dead, as we ourselves breathe and die.

April 12

Arrived at the airport in Santiago. Found a room at the Casahuespedes Sofia near the old Faculty of Philology. Grant money waiting for me at Banco Bilbao. Tomorrow I'll start interviewing people at the university. Very friendly atmosphere in the town. It is an ancient pilgrimage center where the tomb of St. James was found in the ninth century after a shepherd heard celestial music and saw lights in the sky.

The ancient monuments and shrines of this city lead me to think how similar it is to a text. Walking through the streets and alleys I find something of myself in doorways and balconies, roofs and towers I have never seen before. After a brief shower the wet flagstones reflect a light that is as much a part of me as anything I have ever known, though the mists and clouds rolling in on cool drafts from the sea come from a place I have only imagined. Like a geomancer of words I seek the sweet spots, the intersections of sounds and forms that provide the greatest pleasures of being.

April 13

Met with Professor Salsipuede today. He lives in a working class neighborhood not far from the old red light district. One enters a main door in a fairly new but poorly maintained building, and navigates several pieces of discarded furniture before coming to a set of stairs that grow darker with every step. The walls are leeching lime and the door to his apartment is dusted with black mold. When I knocked no one answered, but as I was leaving the building he called out to me somewhat suspiciously. I told him who I was and he invited me back. The apartment had the atmosphere of a mausoleum and seemed to reek of vitamins. The interior hall was so dark it was difficult to find my way at first. Gradually my eyes grew accustomed to the gloom. He was wearing a worn black jacket, a pair of trousers that had been darned in at least a dozen places, a white collarless shirt and a plaid vest. On his left wrist he wore three or four watches (there may have been more beneath the sleeve). His study was lined with chipped and crumbling tiles of dark brown cork. It contained a bicycle, a desk, actually a thick plank resting on two sawhorses, and a battery of wardrobes lined up against the wall, which he gladly opened revealing scores of shoeboxes filled with file cards wrapped in plastic.

"It is my version of the Memory Theater of Giulio Camillo," he exclaimed. "These cabinets contain nothing less than the sum of my research on the works of Atchley. Since you're here to investigate the sources of *Landfall,* let me ask you if you know the significance of the fires the protagonist sees from the summit of the mountain."

I shook my head.

"It's the feast of San Juan," he whispered with discreet satisfaction. "They're a remnant of pagan festivals celebrating the summer solstice. This ties in with the Latin inscription and the gathering of plants. Do you remember the singing he hears while walking in the high fields on his way to the sea?"

"Yes."

"The solo treble from Allegri's 'Miserere.' I know this because he told me."

He closed the cabinet, picked up a violin, and played the first few measures of the piece. I asked him if he would give me a walking tour of the city. He agreed with alacrity. Before we left he cut a piece of bread from a large round loaf sitting on the kitchen table, wrapped it in an embroidered handkerchief, and stuffed it in his pocket for a later lunch.

Salsipuede is a consummate scholar and very likeable. He is eccentric, but more importantly, he is generous. The dissemination of knowledge is his only agenda. As we walked up and down the *ruas* of the city following Atchley's footsteps he revealed an uncanny understanding of the significance of every building and street described by Atchley, as if these places spoke to him, spoke to everyone, about the vital need for contact with the past, and what Atchley has called the "process of life." Death, faith, laughter, love—it's all direct here, as direct as the look one receives from people who pass in the street.

12th or 13th century Latin: "By the order of kings, bishops, elders, all of God, you are warned of excommunication at this castle." Not really a castle, more the ruins of a small tower on top of a peak inhabited by holy men with vestiges of pagan or heretical practices in their worship. A view of Finisterre. That's important as it was the gateway to paradise for Celtic people.

April 14
Saw an interesting piece of sculpture on the side of a church:

a skull and crossbones with the words "COMO TU TE VES, ME VI. COMO TU ME VES, TE SERAS." [As you see yourself, I saw myself. As you see me, so you too will be.]

The Book of Disquiet by Pessoa.

For photo-documentation of the *via lactea* buy Fernando Alonso's *O Camino de Fisterra*. According to Salsipuede, Atchley participated in the field research for this book, particularly in the last stages of the ancient *camino*.

Look up American correspondent of Radio Galicia. Lived in Lubbock [sic]?

April 24
Last week I moved to an apartment in the new part of town. Ermitas promised to keep me supplied with wine from her *finca*. I have the feeling that I've lived all this before. Perhaps it is from reading Atchley. Since moving I don't believe I've talked to anyone.

Every time I go out and walk up the hill to the old part of town and pass beneath its arcades I have the sense that either I am a character in Atchley's narrative or he is a character in mine. How would I know the difference? My narrative could be taking place within his, or his may be nothing without mine. If Atchley were to write a book about me would this be it?

April 25
I have no desire to do anything. I can't bear the idea of reading, and even taking these notes is something I avoid doing for hours. I spent at least an hour today killing the flies in my room. The sun has been shining all day. Perhaps it has sapped my energy. I don't know what has happened to me.

April 28
I was lying in bed thinking about the physical presence of words and the extraordinary trips they take. I imagined the words of "Captive" coming to Atchley on the balcony of the

Foreign Guest House at Shui Li Dian Li in Wuhan and then their journey in a cedar crate to the dusty rail-yards of Hankou where he carried them down the rough cement corridors of a workers' residence to a dimly lit room. A woman in a white cotton shirt was nursing a newborn infant. Her husband emerged from behind a beaded curtain where he was drinking with friends and hoisted the crate onto his shoulder. By the light of a crescent moon he carried it back across the yard, and tossed it into a cavernous freight car, which resonated with the thud of wood on iron. The crate reached the Pearl River by rail and then, by way of Malacca and Said, Tilbury by ship. From Tilbury it was transported to the staid Victorian streets of Clapham by a small white van. After sitting in the hall closet of a narrow flat for two years the words were removed from the crate and rehoused in a stiff cardboard folder. They were revised and added to "The Art of Absence" on a small wooden table beneath a watercolor of Tui by Xulio Rivas and then sent by air cargo to the baked tarmac of Newark where they were cleared and sorted in a large brick building before being delivered to the cubicle of an editor in an office tower in New York. From there they will find their way to a printer in New Jersey and then on to a warehouse in Pennsylvania where they will be dispersed across the country over dozens of interstates by day and night, rumbling along in the holds of semi-trailers until they reach their destinations and are unpacked and arranged in neat piles on lavender tables or slotted on gray shelves under rows of fluorescent lights.

The journeys of the words that make us who we are are not much different. All the words of consciousness must come from or pass through thousands of places in the course of a lifetime. Some change with the places. Others are preserved intact. The reprimands of childhood occur in a rowboat on a lake or on the corner of a busy street. The promises of adolescent love are whispered in the familiar darkness of a public park in a small town in the middle of a continent. Lines of verse slip places into the mind that have never been, places where "light is the lion that comes down to drink."

Just as physical presence is the product of an incomprehensible sequence of conjunctions, so the mind is a combination of all the words it has ever known. We are twice born: into a body and into a language. We have no more ability to determine our language than we have to determine the color of our eyes.

April 30
I don't know what I'm doing anymore. A costly admission, and a fine time to make it. What will the Hollis C. Ellwood Foundation think?

What, after all, does it mean to inquire into the truth of a particular piece of writing, or anything else for that matter? What is the point of arguing whether the world is really there as we know it, or whether reality is mind or mind is language, or whether Atchley's writing is a comment on linguistic idealism? Isn't it all merely delusional? By pursuing "truths" we come to feel that we are progressing toward a higher goal, giving purpose and meaning to our little lives. To argue that we fail to apprehend the truth because of a dogged adherence to faulty constructs or conflicting needs only serves to forestall the inevitable admission that there is no truth.

May 1
What do I really know about Atchley? Wouldn't it be more honest just to admit that I know nothing and invent the author as a work of art? Isn't that what it's all about anyway? Isn't the difference between art and theory one of degree and not substance?

My esteemed colleagues, Atchley woke to a room of lemon daylight, the kind of light he used to see on those cold hard mornings in Hubei when the wind storms of Gansu had filled the sky with yellow dust. He got out of bed and walked down the hallway to the bathroom, which was carpeted and furnished with bright brass fixtures and flawless taupe porcelain. A basket of fruit-scented soap sat on the formica counter. A wreathe with paper flowers hung on the back of the door. Every time he entered the room he thought about smashing it with a sledgehammer, but his daughter would have used the occasion to seek power of attorney. He went to the kitchen and took his shoes out of the microwave where they had been drying, then went out on the back porch. It pleased him to see the grass withering in pale yellow clumps scattering with every breeze across the barren ground. He had refused to run the sprinkler. His daughter had hired a lawn service, but he would sit and drink beer with the men when they came. The conversation helped him ignore the cacophony of neighboring air conditioners and lawnmowers. He often wondered how he had come to this. There had been so many possibilities, so many places where one might grow old among friends.

At night he lies out under the stars and visits all the people he might have been: the one who never wanted anything more than to stay at home in a frame house on a shaded street, the one who wanted to live on a Mediterranean mountaintop with a sympathetic woman from the village, the one who wanted to win the respect of the street-smart in smoky bars with the sharpness of his wit, the one who wanted to wander the Asian hinterlands with nomads who know no law beyond their own horizons.

He would return if he could to the places that have brought a peace to his heart. But he knows that those places only brought that peace at a certain point in time.

[The idea of continuing the story as another character imagines it. Eventually ask who is speaking in the story and who is telling it. "There are only ever two characters—you and me." Then the argument that the character isn't real and shouldn't be allowed to tell a story about a real person. Who is real? Am I not more real than the man standing on a rooftop in a mountain village singing to his child under the moonlight? There are billions of people that you know nothing about, but I have come to exist in your mind. I am forever a part of you. How can you say that I am not real without denying the reality of yourself? And now I can be said to exist in the mind that looks at these words—a voice in the wilderness of an alien mind, slipping down its ivy paths to conjure up a private

42

image. Why the necessity of this compromise with reality? The peculiarity of heart that causes one to live in another vein, always other to what one would be? Spinning, from the furthest recesses of the mind, forms like wind drifts blown by the passions of a moment. And these odd sculptures of the imagination being all we have of true identity. So that to find ourselves we must pass through winter gardens that vanish at the thought of spring.]

May 2
The only way for a work of art to depict life is for that work to change, to be different every time it is experienced, to thrive, as life itself does, on inconsistency and incompletion. On the other hand, is it necessary for a work of art to change when the reader is always changing?

In what way can *Landfall* be considered an account of a life?

May 5
Have I only succeeded in satirizing myself?

May 8
I have decided on a title: *Atchley*. That's the only progress I've made today, unless you can call ripping three paragraphs apart progress.

May 30
Every thought I have, every sentence I write seems to be a lie. The very idea of critical integrity strikes me as absurd. I keep coming back to the same phrases . . . When we consider Atchley's intentions it is important to remember . . . In this study we will examine . . . The principal focus of this work . . . he says . . . she claims . . . he states . . . she argues . . . The subordination of transcendent truths to demotic tastes will permit the interpolation of relativist tendencies . . . The decision to privilege the *Aufhebung* over the quasi-transcendental produces an interminable asymmetry of the deconstructive alterity which escapes mere facticity in a breach of oppositional terms signifying the nondemonstrative suspension of

the trace which is neither the heat of passion nor the marble's chill, give me a thrill . . .

June 1
Sat out on the terrace this evening as the full moon rose over a eucalyptus forest to the southeast.

June 2
I wonder if there is any way out of the framework of thought, the expectations and impositions of an age, of a language, that have brought me to this. I don't care how fantastic, how arbitrary, how disorienting the place I end up, as long as I can find words that spring fresh from intuition and course blindly through the imagination.

I dream of making an imaginative descent to discover the worlds within me, a story with no author, no purpose, a tropological garden whose sun is the light of wonder shining through a haze of convention and intention. [change "tropological garden" cf. Ohm]

It would begin with the following lines:
"Forget about Green. He was merely an expediency within the general strategy. His name is on the cover because that's the way it's done. But he is long gone. The exfoliation of a moment."

June 5
Salsipuede introduced me to Fernando Alonso who showed me what he believes was the final stage of the pilgrim's route on an ordnance survey map complete with notes indicating undocumented petroglyphs, ring-forts, and dolmens. Apparently (1) the route originated in France (2) is five thousand years old and was basically assimilated into Christianity when the Church claimed it had discovered the remains of St. James in a Roman necropolis and built a cathedral on the site. Since the assimilation, this final portion of the pagan trail has largely been ignored. Salsipuede claims this is the most important part of the journey for spiritual rebirth.

June 11
Just read where butterflies can see a fourth primary color. Was trying to imagine what it could be.

June 12
Inventory: knapsack and canteen, bedroll and pancho (it rains a lot here—even in early summer).

1.6093 kilometers in a mile.

June 19
Did a trial run to Mt. Pedroso. Sheaves of hay stacked in green fields. Golden light.

They found his body on the Isle of Ons on the morning of June 23rd. It had washed ashore sometime during the night. I happened to be in Santiago at the time and received a call from Constante at the University to go and identify the body. I took the local ferry out from Sanxenxo the following day. The police were saying that a boat had been reported stolen up the coast at Curra, but as far as I know, no firm connection was ever made.

After the island the first thing I remember is coming upon a group of those that had survived. Everything was growing dark in the dusky flocculence of a midwinter snow, and they were wandering, as if lost, across the coastal plain. Many more would follow. For those in whom the effects were rampant, there was no meddling with cures. And for those who were not in any immediate danger, time proved to be but an illusion of asylum. No return was their refuge and one by one they disappeared.

A fire far out on the horizon would often lead me to find people camped among the open houses of villages or in sheltered fields. I can still see the faces of men and women absorbed in the administration of untried remedies to those among their number who were dying. The children went first, and soon were rarely seen anywhere. After the children, the others, the rest, went in no particular order, with no particular logic. Because the ground was frozen, the bodies were burned in novel rituals adopted for the nonce, and it was my custom, in the beginning, when these occasions were common enough, to stop in the farthest reaches of firelight to watch as gentle currents of night air bore the smoke off over treetops toward the stars, and listen to the songs, so markedly incantatory, that accompanied every ceremony. But as the weeks went by, the sightings of these camps grew fewer and fewer, and I imagined the groups consolidating in order to preserve whatever hope might lie in the collective succor of a community.

Though the direction of my journey roughly followed a gently flowing river eastward, upstream, away from the sea, I found I could move more easily by avoiding the steep ravines that cut the lowland plain, and so, taking to the ridges that flanked the valley, I traveled roads that climbed up hillsides and wound through narrow terraces, where, with little effort, I imagined vineyards thriving in a summer sun. At dusk every evening the sky would clear and crisply set, but by midnight clouds would rise from the valley and race to the inland horizon of darkened peaks and deep recesses. There they would fall into troughs of fog and by morning be gone. Nothing moved or lingered in the air or upon the brown stalks of wild grasses. Underfoot, mixed with the black carpet of fallen leaves, were fetid cinders. Their odor rose from the icy sloughs and brushy streambeds that I crossed to fill the dying forests. I would tell myself that in the depths of the sea the lightless shelves would still be teeming. I pressed my thoughts into any unknown. Rather than consider myself. What power I may have had to confront the hardening knots in my neck and groin, or the darkening veins in my extremities had left me like the fear of god. The damp trees, the damp smoke, the damp skies, and the bodies that had strayed and lay uncollected beneath the odd shrub or propped against a solitary pine came together to form a single image of desolation, a dull gray landscape that I seemed to find before my eyes everywhere I looked. I knew the air would be purer in the mountains without knowing if it mattered.

One night when the unevenness of my path was demanding my full attention, I unexpectedly stumbled upon a large stone wall. Having no choice but to find a way around it, I followed it along some fifty yards, turned a corner, and followed it another twenty or thirty more until I stood before a massive iron gate, which, though badly rusted, opened, permitting entry. Once inside, I saw off at a distance the gray outline of a large house. Light shone from two windows in its upper story. I did not take my eyes from them as I proceeded up the walk. The front door was open and the entranceway was cluttered with leaves and spotted with patches of snow. I went up one flight of stairs in darkness. As I was going up a second, a door opened above me. Light spread and filled the stairwell. An old woman greeted me and led me into a warm room where three other women were seated before a fire. One of them asked if I was the doctor that had been sent for. I told her there were no more doctors. With the other two she returned her gaze to the fire. At the bidding of the woman who had greeted me, I entered another room where a man no older than myself was lying curled in bed. He lifted his hand up and I shook it. His other hand was clasped over his forehead. There was nothing much left of him but his bones and a shrunken covering of skin. Near his waist the white bedspread was stained from a loss of blood. The dark beams of the ceiling pressed low overhead and the wooden floor was warped, meeting the walls at odd angles. Across the room several devotional candles burned on the dresser and a window sill. He asked if I was the doctor. I told him there were no more doctors. He moved his head to one side and said he knew. There was a long pause. I took a step back toward the door. He drew his breath deeply, and then, gesturing toward the window, began to speak: "God almighty first planted a garden," he said, as if quoting a phrase he liked very much. "There were flowers there from every part of the world," he continued, "and varieties for every season. You could read them like a calendar. First the crocuses and hyacinth, then the daffodils. Roses in the summer. The beds neatly trimmed. The lawns nicely cut. Every day new buds, fresh blossoms. Out early on a summer morning to take a walk, or cut a bouquet for the breakfast table. You wouldn't believe it now to see things in such a state." He stopped again. The only sounds were his labored breath and a candle crackling as it died. A slow drop slipped down the misted window. He cast his eyes absently in thought, then looked at me. Fumbling, he reached toward the nightstand and took a thin volume from the pile of books scattered on it. Two slid and fell to the floor. I bent to pick them up, but he waved me off, and began to read: "They being shut up in their houses, the prisoners of darkness, and fettered with the bonds of the long night." Then, following his finger, his eyes moved down the page: "For neither might the corner that held them keep them from fear, but noises as of waters falling down sounded about them, and sad visions appeared unto them with heavy countenances. But they sleeping the same sleep that night, which was indeed intolerable, and which came upon them out of the bottoms of inevitable hell, were partly vexed with monstrous apparitions, and partly fainted, their hearts failing them, for a sudden fear, and not looked for, came upon them. So then whosoever there fell down was straitly kept, shut up in a prison without iron bars. Over them only was spread a heavy night, an image of that darkness which should afterward receive them, but yet were they unto themselves more grievous than the darkness." Here he stopped for the last time and closed his eyes. I wanted to question him about the geography of the mountains, but his strength had evidently been expended. He was wearing a scapular and was fingering one end of it as it lay in the folds of his blanket. The woman who had first showed me in now led me out.

My hands and feet grew whiter and colder. The blood in my arms and legs seemed to thicken and slow. The lumps in my neck had all but closed my throat and had spread to my armpits and from there to my back. Those of my abdomen responded to every digestive movement with searing pain. But at least this came and went. What never ceased was the dull ache behind my eyes. The brightness of daylight caused me exceptional discomfort, and it was only with the coming of extreme fatigue that I could close the lids, as they could not be willfully made to relax. A fear of blindness overwhelmed me.

The streams grew swifter and the trails fewer as I went higher. Snow began to fall one night compounding the prevalence of danger by diminishing visibility. Gathering winds blew it into moving drifts that concealed hazardous footings of loose stones and false surfaces. I could not continue without knowing what lay before me and I could not stop without finding shelter. I set my things on the ground where I stood and circuitously returned to my tracks ten or fifteen yards back. In the loop thus made I passed the night, circling the snowlit course as many as several hundred times. I stepped each step precisely, covering each print again and again, until, after the long hours, morning came with its weak blue light. The storm began to lift an hour or two after dawn and I took advantage of the favorable conditions to make the short but difficult journey down to the river, which I now decided to follow. I arrived at its banks early in the afternoon and continued upstream until I could proceed no further. It narrowed to a width of no more than twenty or twenty-five feet as it flowed through a fissure between two granite bluffs. These, in turn, rose perpendicularly from the surface of the water to a height of not less than two hundred feet. Above that I could see nothing for it was the altitude of the clouds. Evening was beginning to settle in and the snow began to fall once more. The proximity of the clouds, the dim aspect of the bluffs, and the isolating silence of the snow all helped to create a sense of closed space that was as much a part of me as my own thoughts. While yet a trace of light remained I went looking along the riverbank for a suitable place to pass the night and found, a good hundred feet up from the water, a gap in a bed of boulders that quite comfortably accommodated myself and my belongings. With special sticks for rubbing and tinder that I kept wrapped among my things I made a fire, which, once it was going, I fed with damp wood collected from the area. Luckily the smoke rose vertically, and by the strength of its updraft drew in fresh air from the numerous crevices in the rough walls below. I warmed myself and dried my boots and coat while the rocks above me hissed and cracked. When the fire had died down to embers, I roasted several potatoes, and then spread my coat out over the moist sod of the floor, which, thus prepared, should have made a tolerable bed. But sometime early in the night I was roused by what I imagined were lice or fleas feeding on my skin. So insufferable was the sensation that several times I got up and stood over the fire thinking that its smoke might relieve me of the pests. When this had no effect, I stoked the smoldering log-ends for light and stripped off my clothes to discover that much of my body had broken out in a rash that in some places was so severe as to be bleeding. Since I had not noticed it before, I could only conclude that it had come over me in the last few hours and may have been a sign that the

53

general state of my health had taken a turn for the worse. A mental examination of my throat and abdomen confirmed this suspicion. I lay down. The light of the fire grew dim as the flames dropped and went out. I could not sleep, but must have come close, for I remember feeling a sudden jolt and subsequent tremors that, though they frightened me at the time, were doubtless nothing more than my body seizing up on the brink of sleep and my heart pounding in response. Later in the night I half-imagined, half-dreamed that my open abdomen, burning and full of cysts, vividly appeared with its diseased channels and odd growths laid bare. The growths I plucked out one after another, but in their places came a bright red blood that filled and overflowed the open cavity and seeped in streams through the rocks to merge with the river and run outwards toward the sea. I saw myself going back. I passed a city I had not seen before that stood silent and empty in the aftermath of an evening storm. The sun, dropping down from a low black swath of cloud, shone brilliantly on the shattered windows of the tallest buildings, and then disappeared beneath the dark horizon. Below the city the river slowed and widened. Human shapes moved among the silhouettes of trees along the shoreline. I sensed I was being watched as I made my way to the bank and waded through a deep cordon of sedge, but could find no one. The river didn't have far to go before emptying into the sea, and there, somewhere near the point of my departure, I was certain I would find the island. I set out knowing that when I did reach it, morning would be coming on and the sky would slowly warm from its steely blue and the breeze would rise and I would be where I had been so many times before to see it all, and feel the light, the coming light, like a mixture of all the colors of remedy emerging from the dark morphines of my mind. Once again I would set out through the deep wet grasses and climb until I reached a spot high up on a promontory where the stones surface through the thin soil. Dozing there with the sun full on my face, I would feel the weight and awkward assemblage of my bones drawn down as if by the gravity at the bottom of a dream. And with a sense of falling, I would feel the stone pestles grinding and the roots as sieves sifting. The white powder would silently fall, so slowly as to not disturb a single thing. Just to think of it. The snow falling on a sleeping village in a glass curio. Year upon year I am gently taken down. Gently, gently, taken down. But then I heard their voices.

Two or three of them had entered the cave and were lifting me out. Another must have retrieved my boots and coat. The sun was shining brightly, and, for a moment, blinded me. I felt the hesitating steps of those who bore me as they struggled with the burden of my body. When the darkness had cleared from my eyes, I saw sitting off at a distance some twenty or thirty people watching me being laid on the ground. One of them, a young woman, came forward and rubbed the dirt and blood from my skin with snow. Then I lost consciousness. When I came to it was dark and I discovered myself to be wearing my coat and wrapped in a blanket. The young woman was sleeping beside me. It was a bitterly cold night and I lay quiet and still for a long while looking at the stars.

The following morning I awoke to the clatter of tins being scraped of a pastelike meal and the discord of voices cutting across one another, vying for an audience. Everyone seemed to be talking, and no one listening. Except for an old man who sat on the edge of the scene taking things in quietly as he worked his tongue over his toothless gums. After breakfast the women went their separate ways. One began to collect the tins, another to wash them. But the men continued talking. It was not a language I could recognize and they were not a people I could place. Whether they were an indigenous tribe of mountain foragers, or the coherent remnants of a more settled society, I never clearly ascertained. Their world was a potpourri of portents—though with the life gone out of things, they were hard pressed for animated auguries. They looked to the clouds, the river, and the night sky to fill the need. But these were observations I would make in time. On that cold morning it was their generosity that impressed me most: they served me as one of their own. After eating I was brought coffee and tobacco. I revived briefly, then slowly began to sink away again into the sound sleep in which I had passed the better part of the previous day and would pass many more to come.

It was the heaviness and frequency of this sleep, coupled with all that I had seen of pyres and prayers in the past month or two that led me to conclude that my prospects for recovery were not much better than the prospects had been for all of those who had gone before. To make myself ready for what I was certain was coming I trained my thoughts on the subject at hand. I imagined every means of going, considered every idea of the instant. I pictured, for example, the drowning man who, after rising for the third time, makes his last breath of water. I felt myself in the fall of the climber who drops through the sky to a narrow grave of snow. I saw the light of the mind passing down its hall of mirrors seeking from all that it has lived what it had chanced upon before and longs to chance upon again. I was at it until the moment of sleep. I was at it upon awakening. And while I was at it, I waited. The others waited. We waited several weeks. But I did not die. I recovered. My mood changed.

Within a week or ten days of the first signs of improvement, I was ready to travel, but only in a most desultory fashion, for I was frequently hobbled by nervous fits. The soles of my feet would become painfully cold and even numb if I stood on them for very long, and when I sought to exercise my limbs too vigorously, they would go into strange convulsions that left me both exhausted and perplexed. Though the woman who had been taking care of me and the old man and a few other members of the group showed great patience toward me, the rest, undoubtedly because of my lameness, ventured off on their own. In each case this was preceded by an acrimonious exchange between those who left and those who stayed. Angry eyes fixed on me. Of those who left, a few returned famished or maimed, but that did not deter them, once they had appeased their appetites or mended themselves, from leaving again. For this reason I was never sure just how many of us there actually were. Though their rashness and the lack of introspection that accompanied it preserved them much better than could be expected by staying their minds from the tendency to advance their disorders with worry, it exposed them to the increasing risks of our solitude. We later discovered the remains of one man at the bottom of a ravine and of another, who we assumed had starved to death, along our path. The folly of this rashness was, at first, magnified in my eyes by my inability to understand the language of these people. But even when I began to make some sense of what they were saying, my point of view changed very little.

When it came time to set out on our way, we returned downstream about a mile to where there was a wooded hollow whose gentle slope offered us an agreeable, if somewhat indirect route to the top of the ridge, which we crossed over late in the afternoon. We came down a little and then stopped at a place where we could see what lay before us. The river, reflecting the sky from the shadows of the plain, was like running silver, and on either side of it rose the mountains I had been seeing for the better part of my journey. The ridge, with the exception of the chasm cut by the river, stretched from the mountains on the left to those on the right, and as a result of this, the valley nestled below could not have been more isolated. We ate hurriedly as the cold winds picked up suddenly after sunset, and spent the night under the partial shelter of a stone ledge. The next day we descended to level ground. Along the river the earth was frozen, but free of snow, and we made considerable progress for several days before stopping to camp on the site of a crumbling stone tannery built astride a quick clear stream. There we each had our own box-like pit, which, filled with dry leaves, became our beds.

The first warm weather of spring swept through the valley with singing winds and sweet rains. The shelves of ice on the stream melted. The pits grew musty and the footpaths muddy. We searched the area for watermills where we hoped to find grain or even flour, but for several days no one strayed very far. There was nothing much for anyone to do. Some sat in their pits passing the time in silence. But the more animated were up, gathered in a corner, exchanging words of anger, or at least exaggerated annoyance. This was a regular part of their social behavior, and though it rarely came to anything, it made me think that I must have come from a people more accustomed to living quietly, a people who had listened, as I listen, more to the vagaries of thought. One rainy evening I approached the pit of the woman in whose care I had been, intent on learning something of the language that surrounded me. When I tried to speak to her, a man who had been watching from an adjacent hole cut me off. He drew his thick fingers through his beard and with little trouble communicated his aversion to the plan. I moved away to a back window and did not repeat my attempt.

On a calm and cloudless morning shortly after the rains had let up I went for a walk through a stand of walnut trees along the stream above the tannery. The day was typical of early spring and I remember thinking how the bare trees had yet to deny the prospect of a fragrant green summer. But suddenly, without the slightest warning, I received a sharp blow to the back of my head. I dropped to the ground and into darkness. When I began to come round, every thought, every intention, flew from any focus into the general grip of pain that possessed me, and it was several minutes before I realized through whatever agency it may have been, that something was wrong below. I hurried down with as much haste as I could summon and stopped only when I had come within sight of the tannery. The man who had checked me some nights before emerged carrying something blue and dripping blood in his outstretched hands. It gave off a wisp of steam as he held it up to the morning light. Then he turned, opened a barrel of salt and dropped it in.

As I entered the gloomy den of our camp, the old man rose from his place before the fire and said something with awkward gestures of obliged concern. The woman's body was dragged from her pit. Her eyes were open and her clothes were torn and soaked with blood. She was placed on a pile of damp logs, and in the night they tried to burn her, but the wood did not light. The next morning a plot of earth was loosened, more plowed than dug, and her body, sprinkled with salt, was covered with dirt. As the earth showered over her unflinching eyes and tamped her shining hair under its rough hold, I felt a sadness I had forgotten I could feel.

Motivated more by fear than by vengeance or a sense of justice, I decided to do something about the man who had attacked me. The afternoon following the burial I came across a thin but sturdy length of rope. My plans were fairly simple, and once they had been made, it was just a matter of waiting. Nightfall came and I waited a little longer. Then, an hour or so after the fire had been abandoned, I was ready. I crawled out of my hole and crossed the narrow surfaces of the upright stones that formed the walls of the pits to a level platform near the doorway. It appeared that everyone was asleep. I tied one end of the rope to a large wheel that had once opened a sluice gate. The other I tied into a slip knot and tossed over a beam directly above my sleeping victim. I let it down until it almost touched him, and then crawled back across the pits until I came to his. He was a big man and slept soundly, nevertheless slipping the noose under his head was a very delicate operation. When I had finished, I crawled back to the platform still wondering if what I was doing would work. I fixed my mind on something else, something pleasant, it seems, like sunshine sparkling on the surface of the sea, and gave the wheel several quick turns. Less the low groan of the rope across the beam, he went up silently. I inserted a board through the spokes to hold him where he was and sat down for a rest. The old man must have been awakened by the noise, as I saw the top of his head rise above the rim of his pit in a posture that indicated he was looking at the body swinging mere feet from his brow. But he never so much as glanced in my direction, and was soon down again, probably thinking it wise to leave well enough alone. Twenty minutes is the amount of time I associate with hanging, and after reckoning a good twenty had passed, I slowly released the rope to its charge, slipped it from the wheel, and went to retrieve both it and the body. The heaviness of a body when freshly dead is greater than what one who is not acquainted with them might think, and it was only with considerable exertion that I managed to lug this one outside and down to the river, which carried it away effortlessly in the swirling night of its vernal waters.

We recommenced our march upstream uneventfully one morning some days later when the sun was still behind the mountain peaks. Each member of our dwindling band was laden with an allotment of community property that included bottles, candles, potatoes, tools, bowls, and the like in proportion to his or her strength. In addition to this we each carried as much personal property as we could. I kept a tin of aspirin and a jar of vitamins. Vade mecums of a sort. My needs were very limited and I knew that anything I might eventually want could be found in a house somewhere along the way. Though our economy was humble, it was advantageous to all. Certainly no one suffered more than his or her share of hunger.

As the days passed, the cries and utterings that made up the conversations of my fellow travelers went through a subtle metamorphosis. That is, they lost the appearance of a brute nomenclature and took on the seductive sympathy of a human language. In the beginning I learned "yes," "no," "hello," "good-bye," "wait," oaths, exclamations, and a few numbers. These came rather easily as did words like "water," "food," "fire," "rain," and "river," which, rude sounds that they seemed, were quite a useful stock when accompanied by gestures that made up for a want of pronouns and verbs. Of course the verbs "I want," "I have," "eat," "sleep," "come" and "go," and "I'm going to," fundamental as they are, were not far behind. But here I reached a plateau in my progress, and learned no more than a word a day during our stay in the tannery. Only so much can be done with words sifted from contexts, and contexts, apart from those conveying my vital needs, were luxuries beyond my ambition. Now, however, as we began our second sustained march, some innate faculty had me speaking the language of these people, often without my realizing it. But here my difficulties did not end. No sooner did I become modestly accomplished in this language, than I noticed it being used by my companions to portray not what they saw, but what, quite plainly, they wanted to see. Obviously this was not done all the time, otherwise I would have learned the negative of a positive reality, and by way of consistency, made perfect sense. Something like the mind righting the image of inverting spectacles. So when we happened upon barren tracts of rain-scarred land, they were described as green fields blown by a west wind under a soft summer sun. It wasn't long before I too was depicting a ridge of seared oak as the edge of some arcady, or a dripping evening sky as resplendent with color. My attempts pleased the others to no end and caused them to encourage me with thoughtful nods and even embellishments of their own.

Eventually the descriptions lengthened into vignettes, and the vignettes, in turn, lengthened into stories, severely testing my rudimentary use of the language. I went from describing clouds as red to inventing scenes of life to fill the empty yards and lanes of the farming villages through which we passed. Though my choice of words would have been much more limited, I would have tried to present a picture similar to the one that follows:

Wood pigeons are milling about the chimney of an abandoned farmhouse. Smoke is rising from garden fires into the late afternoon. A church bell tolls the hour. A woman standing in the doorway of a house watches a man lead a horse from a barn. The man, a blacksmith, lets go of the horse and closes a gate behind him. He waves to the woman, and walks down a narrow lane whistling to himself. He stops on a bridge in the middle of the village and drops a ball of horsehair he has collected from his shirt into the water. Drops of rain begin to fall, sounding heavily on the leaves of the chestnut trees. The young glover's wife comes running beneath the verdant canopy of the lane with a white hat in her hand. The blacksmith turns to look as she crosses the bridge and watches her as far as the manor gate where she disappears behind a hedgerow. Beyond the village, beyond the ripening apple orchard, where the river turns to the north, men are cutting hay in golden fields ahead of the rain they scent coming over the western slopes.

My companions, critically mute, would be contentedly eyeing the western clouds for any sign of gentle rain.

That summer the world was there as my naked will would have it in a dream. Such was the transparence of my telling. Perhaps it was because the stories came as such relief that the time went by so quickly. I imagined their effect on my mind like that of sunlight in a garden, bringing forth forgotten life. But for the others it was different. They were looking for something else, something more, something to believe in. For them each tale demanded another, and the first was taken to be the fact that gave credence to the second, and the second, the third, and the third, the fourth, and so on, until they had themselves not just a story, but a history. And sometime toward the end of the summer one such history appeared that overshadowed all of those that had come before it, one which, drawing on our deepest fears and needs, ultimately had to go unfinished:

One evening an ancient, unknown figure approaches us on the path. He is wearing a white robe, and his face is surrounded by a white halo of hair and a long white beard. He speaks briefly, directing us to continue our course up the river, and then vanishes into the growing darkness of the lifeless woods. Speculation follows as to his identity, and what, if anything, more we are to expect. He next appears at night. We see him coming at a distance, down from the east. He stops and speaks. The burden of this terrible land will soon end, he promises. You will leave this desert one day and the cold winds that descend from the mountains will be far behind you. You have faced the winter, now ready yourselves for what must follow. He says nothing more, and, cutting through the woods, goes beneath the western stars. A week passes. Once more he approaches in darkness, but this time he comes in the hour before dawn. There is a land yet to the east, he says, where these waters rise and the morning sun emerges from just beyond the distant hills. No winter blasts will drive you to shelter. No summer heat will scorch a fruitless earth. Lives of waiting, the sufferings, dissolve as you awaken, to like first wakening, to a countryside in bloom. As the low sun brings the green fields to a fullness of life, you are one, in response, with all around you. Shadow is of another world and even the darkness deep within your bodies will be banished by a return to light.

But, of course, no summer came. Winter, in fact, was on its way. This, however, did not deter them. The history went on. Reasons multiplied for our continued hardships, and any shortcomings found responsible were clearly our own. Loss of faith was first among them. When it became evident that the white-robed figure would not return, it was because, as one faction had it, there was nothing more he could tell us, or because, as the other faction had it, we had been loath in some way to seek what he had promised. These points of view became tenets in no time at all, and we were soon in the throes of a schism. The three, I believe there were three, who subscribed to the latter opinion, crossed the river and set out due east expecting, before it was too late, to find either the figure of the history or the land he had spoken of. The rest, five in number, including myself, maintained our somewhat circuitous course coinciding with that of the river. It was not long before the mountains were capped with the first snows of the season, and the three, not surprisingly, were never heard from again.

With each of us conscious of the danger another split in the group would bring, it was natural that nothing more was said concerning the figure of the history. But this did not mean he was not on our minds, nor that the stories we sub-stituted were anything other than stories of him. Shunting our words thus from their subject inspired an uncommon latitude of fancy, and on the long marches of those lean days, one could hear descriptions of most anything and everything, short of the unimaginable. It was for this reason that when the others began to speak of the twin towers and imposing walls, I did not trouble myself to raise my head to confirm the fiction experience had taught me to expect. So a little later on, when I next happened to look up, it came as something of a surprise to find myself in the immediate precincts of a large abbey. Surrounded by gray clusters of willows and elms, it stood on high ground overlooking a shallow bend in the river, while behind it, at a distance of no more than half a mile, the facing slopes of the valley closed in to a point just shy of convergence. I stopped and watched the others gradually make their way down the final stretch of the road. Before me spread the russet fields of last year's uncut hay. Moist cliffs above the river glistened in the afternoon light. I sat on a solitary stump by the wayside until the sun went down and the deep colors of twilight began to edge outward from the eastern sky. The moon was there too, but had not yet cleared the looming summits that grew somber against its golden light. Flickering in the northern tower of the church, the candle of one of my companions caught my eye, and then the valley filled with the lilting clamor of bells. I rose, refreshed for the moment, and began the final portion of the day's journey more in the light of the moon than the sun. The road went no further than a few hundred feet before terminating at a series of stairs I had seen the others take. The narrow passage was bordered on left and right by dense thickets of broom, and because it doubled as the channel of a small stream, I had to undergo a thorough soaking of my boots and trousers before finally coming to a gatehouse and open ground.

The bells had since stopped ringing and the only sound was of the river's steady flow, which resonated in the unseen corners and countless hollows of the several walls and buildings. In the clear moonlight I imagined the scattered stones of the churchyard to be the cold bones of a mythical beast fallen from its wars with heaven. The church itself was large, and as I stood in the portal and looked around, I thought it seemed to contain a night unto itself. My four companions had gathered together in the chancel, forming a bright anchor to the dancing shadows thrown around them from a dozen burning candles. The smell of beeswax mingled with that of damp stone. I went toward them down a side aisle drawing alongside a broad column and peering into the weak light. The old man was holding a crude purse in one hand while the other alternated between rounding its shape and picking bits of dried debris from its lining. The importance of what he was doing was reflected in the fastness of his mien. I watched him work for several minutes until he removed his hand and the supple leather sank back upon itself, then glancing to his face, I found myself the object of his scrutiny. He signaled that I should join them, and when I did he gave me the purse to examine for myself. It was lighter than I had expected it to be. Taking it back he demonstrated the purpose of the cord he had threaded through its neck by wrenching it tightly. A short man, he came only to my shoulders, and as he inspected his handiwork, I inspected him. I don't know what I was looking for. Something to distinguish us, to draw the line more clearly. His gaze moved upward, climbing through the darkness, and then settled once again on me. He prompted my approval with a nod, and with a nod I gave it. For a moment he searched my eyes, and then stretched out his arm as if inviting me to take my place beside the others. I must have seemed somewhat reluctant for he repeated the gesture and then slipped away along the wall of the south transept. I mounted the steps of the altar just as a candlestick was raised aloft. It gleamed an instant as a grip was taken, a finger adjusted, and then came swiftly down to shatter the glass case of the abbey's reliquary. From the folds of faded satin, the shards and splinters, four small bones were plucked. A space was cleared and the candles were moved in close. Our companion best described as burly hunched his broad shoulders over the altar and with an improvised stylet began to cut notches and designs into the rounded surfaces of the bones. Sebaceous lumps covered his face and hands, and every few minutes a palsy swept his back in such a way as to hike the sleeves of his jacket up his wrists. His eyes were dry and red and his rotten teeth shown like cusps of gritty ice. At his side, tending the candles and holding the bones in place were the other two members of our group, a man and a woman, who assisted unassumingly. Just as the carving was being completed, the old man returned. He took the bones, now etched with tiny chevrons, crenels and half-spirals, and tossed them into the purse. As we left the altar and filed toward the portal, he went ahead and pushed back the two timber doors to allow as much light to enter as possible. Then we turned a pew around and sat facing outward, waiting for I knew not what. Sleep came and went as the hours stole by. From the others I heard nothing, not so much as a sigh or yawn. Everything outside from the fields and trees to the walls and steps was bathed in whiteness. The light inched its way across the threshold and over the smooth stones of the floor. I measured its slow advance by keeping a watch on certain lines and cracks until they broke from darkness. And when the moon, like a lazy eye, finally dropped beneath the portal arch, I could almost feel the west ascending. The old man rose, stepped forward, and placed himself squarely in its path. Then he turned to face us. The contrast of the light from behind obscured his features by casting him in a uniform gray the color of wet ash. His head moved slightly from side to side, as if rocking to an inner rhythm. The others got up and circled the marble font that stood in the center aisle. They lit candles and set them on its rim. The old man's eyes glimmered as they moved back and forth, from left to right, right to left, searching the empty space around us. His head inclined forward, a little turned to one side, his ear intent on the stillness. When the moment was right, he removed the purse from his sash, emptied the bones into the shallow basin of the font, picked them up, blew on them, shook them in the hollow of his cupped hands, and let them fall. Then he looked up, toward the ceiling, and, in a low tone, called out for some response. A few minutes later he whispered something to himself, collected the bones a second time, dropped them into his purse, and restored it to his sash. Before the woman could finish pinching the candles out, he was down the front steps and hurrying across the yard. The rest of us followed him to the porch and watched him from there. He went all the way out to the perimeter wall where he quickly went to work gathering twigs and small branches from the ground around what appeared to be a row of laurel. When his arms were full he came back up toward the church, stopped alongside a large tomb, and dropped his bundle on its lid. He arranged the sticks to form a broad circle, placed the bones at its center, and set it alight. Bending round and round with the breeze, the flames burned for several minutes, until, their fuel spent, a burst of wind blew them out. Then the old man took each bone, washed it with water from a blue phial, and rubbed it dry with a white cloth. When he had finished with the last one, we went back inside the church. The moon had slipped behind the western mountains and the hint of light at the chancel windows was that of morning. The others went no further than the font, but I continued down the center aisle until I came to the rail around the altar. The mere approach of dawn marshaled new perspectives. It was as if the familiarity of the hour could make common even that which had seemed most foreign. The statues staring from their smooth eyes, the slender pillars soaring into graceful arches, the gold brocade of the altar skirt were all transformed. No less was the old man's voice, which, contained within the walls of cold stone, sharpened to a clearer timbre. I went out a door in the south transept and discovered the abbey's cloister. At the center of the neat grass quadrants was a fountain that still flowed. I stopped for a moment and felt its spray, carried by the breeze, fall lightly on my face. The sky above was radiant, and the air, it seemed, was growing colder. On the western side of the arcade was an open passage that led down a dark hallway to a one-room apartment set off by itself. Here I made myself at home. I unlatched the windows, gave the sheets and blanket a shake, and went to bed. I had hoped to sleep, but there was too much daylight in my blood. And hunger scraped my stomach. Merely shutting my eyes had to suffice. It was almost the same, almost as sound. Yet the hours passed so slowly.

By noon I was up and about, wandering in and out of rooms, trying to get a sense of the life of those who had been here before. It wasn't difficult. They had fled with such haste that whatever they had been doing at the time had been left undone. In the refectory, for example, the long oak tables were still set, and shriveled trout lay like small stones on the dull platters. I tried to imagine what it had been that had driven them out, had caused their desperate rush to collect what was precious and make for open spaces, but there seemed to be no answer. I went outside to see what the grounds looked like in the daylight and found a silver aspersorium that had been lost in a deep tangle of vetch. In the bake house, the brew house, the smith's workshop, everywhere I went, there were the same signs of impetuous flight. Benches were overturned, coins dropped, curtains torn. When I came to the barns I found the animals dead in their stalls. Their bulky carcasses had collapsed like tents to the ground and their

hardened skins were drawn drum-tight over disordered pro-
trusions of bones. I had come far enough for the moment.
Woozy from a lack of sleep and not a little hungry, I wound
my way back through the desolate gardens and walks to the
church where I found my companions sitting around a gray
heap of embers and ashes in the center aisle just beside the
font. We fixed a lunch consisting of our usual regimen of
porridge and coffee, and as we ate I told them what I had
seen in the rest of the abbey, and pictured the hasty departure that must have taken place. They did not seem at all
surprised. It was as if they had expected as much. When we
finished eating, the conversation turned to the numerous
stones in the yard, and on the hunch that their decorations
might yield something of interest, we decided to go out and
have a closer look at them. We examined at least a dozen of
the most elaborate grave-markers before concluding that they
were all pretty much the same, and fairly ordinary at that.
There were sunbursts and quarter moons, and occasionally,
stylized flowers, but these could be found in any churchyard.
Then, as we were rounding the northwest corner of the church,
we saw, standing off on its own, a large granite cross. It rose
to a height of ten or twelve feet, and even from a distance we
could see it was covered with figures that, however deeply
wrought, were badly weathered. Those of the upright portion,
the only ones that were clear enough to read, were divided
into three frames and we were soon studying each of them
assiduously. The highest depicted the struggle of a man clutch-
ing a post or pillar while being torn from it by a creature that
appeared to be part bird, part reptile. In the next one down
there were four bishops or abbots standing with their crosiers.
And the lowest, which was only just discernible, presented a
row of people cowering beneath a sky in flames. I took the
carvings to represent important scenes from the legends or
beliefs of those who had been here before, and not as something I could hope to understand. But my companions, on the
contrary, were all too willing to offer their own explanations
wherever one was lacking. The burning sky they said they had
experienced themselves, the figures holding the crosiers they
reasoned were among the early prelates of the abbey, and the

pillar they agreed was the only other stone of any size in the area, an enormous menhir pitched on a swell of land just inside the southern wall. Once they had completed their inspection of the frames, their attention, as might be expected, turned to this stone, and on surveying it they felt their reading of the cross supported by the five small holes in its side, shoulder high and fitting the spread of their outstretched hands. They needed no more convincing than that. This was the grip of a man, they said, and this was the spot where the struggle that could be seen on the cross had taken place. As we walked back to the church in the low angled light of afternoon, a discussion ensued over the details of their interpretations, but electing not to participate in the exchange, I returned to the room where I had spent that morning and went to bed.

The weeks that followed our arrival at the abbey were marked by a daily routine that was simple and unvarying. We ate. We slept. We passed the hours telling stories. There was nothing to distinguish one day from the next. But then something else began to happen. Something that would eventually spell the end of much that had been familiar in the land, the river, and the sky. At some point a drought started. In the beginning no one noticed. There was nothing to notice. The last rain wasn't thought to be the last when it fell. But as the weather turned warmer things began to change. The river went quiet. The earth cracked. Soil from the garden slipped through our fingers like sifted flour. Then the spring winds came. Rolling banks of dust were lifted from the surface of the land and left suspended in layered sheets above the horizon. Dull haloes appeared around the moon, and in the evenings, just after sunset, the sky assumed a fading green candescence. In time the river went dry. What did not evaporate was absorbed in stagnant pools. The only water we had to drink was from the deepest well and was acrid and flush with clay sediment. The worst thing though was the driven sand. Clear windows were hazed through its effect. Shutters were pocked and splintered and often gave way. And though we rarely went out, when we did, we were forced to cover our faces with damp rags. But finally, after several months, perhaps the entire length of the summer, cooler air came and the winds died down. The nights grew absolutely still. It was like this for a week, and for a week we forgot the elements could be so hostile. Then, in a languid, cream-white sky, pale brown clouds began to build. Breezes sharply scented with moisture gently stirred. The sun quickly disappeared. The rains that followed were, both in spectacle and destruction, every bit equal to the drought they succeeded. In twelve hours the winterbournes were gushing; in twenty-four the river was halfway up the lawn. On the second day, in the overcast light of noon, I stood at a chancel window and watched as the ragged edge of the bank retreated towards me. Bright chunks of exposed earth slid into the water and dissolved in an instant. Willows that lined the esplanade toppled one after another, cleaving the brown currents, and vanishing beneath a rusty froth. From a broken window in the clerestory I could see that the perimeter wall had been washed out in several places and that the mill and a number of animal pens had disappeared except for the faint outlines of their foundations. In less than a week the water rose to cover the floor of the nave, but the church and cloister were solidly anchored on a plinth of stone, and we felt secure enough staying on in the warming chamber where we had taken shelter during the long months of the drought. For a while we idled our time away with little or nothing to interrupt the succession of empty hours. Then, toward the end of the second week of rain, when the water was waist-high around the altar, the woman in our group came down with an intractable ague. Her teeth rattled ceaselessly. Her cold and purple flesh had the look of bruised marble. At night we took turns sleeping by her side. We did what we could. Tied by a rope to an iron bar in the window of the chapter house, I waded out to the infirmary where I recovered a score of gallipots and a basketful of herbs. Together we hauled a vat up from the brewery, and to arrest the advancement of her sores, we bathed her in a solution of carbolic acid. Flowers and leaves, dry as dust, were sprinkled in her soup and to drink we gave her infusions of bark. When she slept well, or when her eyes brightened, we continued with the same treatment. Then, just when her improvement was a hope to be entertained, she became the victim of violent nightmares. Because she had been sleeping close to the fire, we first attributed them to its heat. But when we moved her away from it, her torments continued and became increasingly vocal. Convinced that the fire was not to blame, I started to move her back, only to be met by the protests of the others who still argued that there was something in it that troubled her, something we could not see that was preying on her as the weakest of our number. They became more and more adamant and then decided to do without a fire altogether. But here I imposed the authority that was mine by virtue of a slight advantage in health and told my three fellows that the last word on the subject belonged to the woman alone. They had no choice but to agree. The afternoon of the following day, when she was awake and peaceful, the question was put to her. I promised her that if she wanted a fire, she would have one. She did not. The fire was extinguished. That evening as I lay in bed I felt the cold creep up my spine and cradle my head in its icy fingers. I heard coughing all through the night. In the morning the woman was dead. There was no way we could bury her, so her body was set adrift where the currents were strongest. I climbed the tower steps and watched it as far as the gatehouse, where a heavy volume of water rushed it through, westward on its course.

A few days later the rain stopped. The floodwaters subsided in a week. I cleared a path through the brush that lay deposited at high water, and when the mud had dried enough to support my weight, I decided to go out and have a look around. The first place I went was the orchard. All that remained of it was a scattering of trees riding high off the stony ground on the tangled webs of well-scoured roots. A little further along was a meadow, reduced, as might be expected, to a layer of gray bedrock. In fact there was very little left to distinguish one stony plot from the next. It seemed that every grain of soil had been washed down to the black mire of the plain below where great piles of timber rose up like fringing reefs in the coastal waters of a barren continent and countless bubbling pores were feeding brown streams that flowed with vein-like symmetry into the trapped backwaters of the river.

71

We were now down to the last four men. The sun stayed hidden, the cold continued, and still we had no fire. The threat was not forgotten. As soon as the water had receded, I returned to my original lodgings. Once the walls and floor had been washed and the mud removed from drawers and shelves, I began to stock the place. First I brought in a barrel of water and a large sack of flour, and then, dismantling the loft of a small barn, I salvaged a cord of dry fuel, which I stacked just inside the door. When the stores were adequate for the siege I expected, I sealed myself off in the apartment and lit a fire. The smoke was slow to diffuse through the still air and two hours passed before I was conscious that the others had arrived. I listened to them whispering as they made their way around the corner of the building and back again. Though timorous, they were desperate, and when the balance of their fear had shifted, they began to rap on the shutters with stout clubs. The clamor they were making was more an agitation than a threat, but it had to be answered. I took a sharp stake from the fire, and stepping outside, thrust it into their faces with a rancor I hoped would impress them more effectively than discourse. Their retreat was hasty, absolute, and proved by time to be permanent. Once content that all objections had been allayed, I settled in to enjoy the comforts of my hearth. My bones warmed, my feet tingled, and I felt my face redden. Oak chairs and chests emerged from deep shadows, and dozens of small fires glimmered in the dozens of small panes in the doors of the bookcase. But there was little to do. The first day passed. Then the second. Then the third. And I sat on in the same place, in the same plump chair, before the fire imagining, day after day, that time would eventually come to an end. Sometimes I would exercise, or count the stones in the wall, or make lengthy calculations, adding, subtracting, and multiplying arbitrary numbers just to make the hours pass. But as the weeks went by, my pile of wood grew smaller and I became restless. It must have been early spring when I finally opened the door and went out, as I remember being startled by the gingery scent of earthy freshness. Half-blind and dizzy from the light, I walked along the cloister's arcades, going into rooms, looking for the others. From the upper gallery I descended by way of the night-stairs, glanced into the warming chamber, found nothing, and continued the search through the nave and chancel. The first indication I had that anyone was still around was the unpleasant odor coming from somewhere near the front of the church. As I approached I could hear someone crying quietly and was led by this low sound to find the old man tucked in a narrow space behind one of the portal's open doors. He was curled up in an agonized state and badly soiled. I picked him up and carried him in my arms to the warming chamber where I built a fire and filled the vat with water. He gazed at me with the sad eyes of a small child. Resignation was the fact of his body's knowing. I bathed him and burned his clothes. Then I dressed him in a robe, gave him something to eat and began to question him about the others. "Dead," he said, "all the others dead. From whatever it is." After some moments of silence he asked if I would take him to the fragment of forest that remained on the back slope of the abbey. In itself the request was not unreasonable, but as we were crossing the yard, he added to it a series of others, the execution of which took us along the many passageways and paths of the grounds to see the standing stone and the cross and the western view, until I tired. Then we knelt on the floor of the church and sang a kind of hymn to the naked walls. This went on for several minutes and when he stopped, I could sense there was something portentous in the silence. We left the church quickly, and holding the old man's arm around my neck, I half dragged him across the rocky stretch of terrain that had once been one of the gardens and down a slope to the copse. There I sat him on a stone and leaned him back against the hollow trunk of an oak. Then, lifting his ankles, I turned him, as he preferred, to face the east. Below us, on the left, he could see the river emerging from the mountains and veils of cloud hanging over the valley. Above was a low gray ceiling, unbroken but for a small opening where a pink blank of sky shone through like a backdrop at the end of the world. After he had looked the scene over for a little while, he asked me if I would bury him beneath a pile of stones. I agreed, thinking he meant afterwards, but a moment later he intimated with a nod that he was ready for me to begin. I went ahead and complied with his request, though I was careful to arrange the stones in such a way as to spare him the greater part of their weight. As the level of the cairn rose to his chin, the darkness spreading through the grove became palpable. And, perhaps knowing that what little was left would be the last light he would see, the old man wanted to be sure his voice still sounded in a world outside his mind. But now he did not sing. It was more like praying. With manifest reverence he addressed the figure from the history. He spoke to him as to one present and asked him to make a place for him far from his unhappy remains. When I set the final stone before his eyes, he stopped short. The spell was canceled. Later in the night, after a long silence had been observed, he told me he saw himself being drawn feet first into the freezing orifice of a blue chamber. It was the last thing he would say. Toward morning his breath grew labored and at length he struggled with the closing of his throat. Then something seemed to break within and he was gone. The clouds overhead parted briefly to reveal the shimmering depths of the dawn sky and a clear cold field of stars.

This was the last death I would witness, and only now, after giving it much thought, did I begin to see nature's purpose in all of this, that she was working to heal herself of man. And I, as the last to come of all of those who had gone before, was to be burdened with her double fate of death and extinction. My existence bore within it the seed of her anathema and I could already envision the conquest of my half-exposed body in her rich black soil: my teeth sown like stars in its firmament and my bones tossed up by the slow pitch of its drifting surface. I often asked myself why I had outlasted the others, what had happened in the beginning, and all the rest. I knew I would never come to any conclusions, but I couldn't help wondering, couldn't help trying to work my time and loneliness away with these and other mysteries. I had to keep my mind occupied. Something was beginning to get at it, something in my room I could not see but heard. It was like the sound of stones being strained or snow pressed by a footfall. It came only at night, and then only at ten to fifteen minute intervals. Attempting to locate its source I sometimes stood on my bed with an ear cocked to the ceiling, but to no avail. It was behind the walls or buried among the rafters. It was the ground shifting beneath the floorboards or the stones contracting in the coolness of the night. At first there was no shortage of explanations. Then one evening I noticed that something had changed. I sat on the bed and listened. I lit a candle and sat in the chair. I studied the shadows in the corners. Hours passed and I heard nothing. I pulled down the blankets slowly, silently, slipped beneath them and blew out the candle. I finally fell asleep, and there it was. Before I was even aware of being awake, I felt the blood rise stinging to the surface of my skin, and I was soon wet with perspiration, but I did not move. For the remainder of the night I lay awaiting its next approach, and then by dawn it had gone the way it had come. I filled the fireplace with stones, then moved the bookcase to brace the door and the wardrobe to reinforce the window. But whatever it was continued undeterred to wake me and to linger in the darkest hours of the night. I was too frightened to burn a candle or close my eyes or turn my head. I kept myself completely still, breathing with quiet constraint through my mouth. I could hear it moving, crossing from door to chair to table, and coming close. Night by night I tried to piece together what it was. And night by night we waited. It for my return to sleep, and me for slivers of daylight to pierce the darkness of my room. At first what sleep I managed came just after dawn, but in time the broken intervals began to extend into evening. I knew the rest I was missing would catch up with me. I sensed the night would soon arrive when, dulled by fatigue, my guard would falter, and all the waiting would be at an end. My raw nerves were fired with fresh apprehension. I could no longer tell sleep from wakefulness, the spasms of fear in my back from the cold touch I was certain would come. Then I lost track of everything. Night was day, day, night. The days, weeks, the weeks, days. I remembered nothing. I don't know how long I was like this. But finally it came. That I remember. That I can't forget. Finally I woke to find myself wrapped tightly in a blanket and backed against a wall. My hands and feet were bleeding. The

75

wardrobe was overturned. The shutters were ripped from their hinges, and the glass gone from the window. I climbed through the splintered casements and fell on my hands. Stars were shining. I pulled the blanket over my shoulders and ran across the yard to the northern tower. I circled round, circled up, by the stone steps to a platform just below the bells. I knew it even in the dark. Hanging overhead were windspun plumes of cobwebs. The floor was littered with the bones of small birds. I crept to an embrasure where I propped myself up and looked out. The view was good, though the opening narrow. I watched, still not sure what I was looking for, but knowing it would be the only thing that moved. Furtive, half-hidden by a corner, half-seen in a glance, it was certainly there. The others had had no doubt. It was carved on the cross. It had always been there, patient, in the mountain forests, and now it had returned. I looked hard on every object, every shadow that might conceal it. I could see most of the stones of the main yard and the statue of the saint that had been hauled outside to oblige its intervention during the deluge. Its hands were lifted to the night. Its human form was far from reassuring. I listened for the river, but, slowed in the muds left by the rain, it could no longer be heard. The only sound was of fitful drafts honing songs around the bells. In the distance the flats of the valley were blue beneath the moonless sky. The stars were red and green and trembling. Somewhere they were shining on the sea. Somewhere they were shining on the island, now more a promise than a memory. I decided, let come what may, that I had had enough. I cupped my hands around my mouth and called out. Emboldened, I raised my voice and shouted again, and watched. Then, quickly, I felt my way to the stairs and down to the portal. I slipped a metal bar from the door and clenched it tightly in my hand. Turning as I went, I swung the bar around me and stepped into the yard. What I wanted now was open space. I had had enough of shelters. I wanted to see what was coming on all sides. I walked across the yard, climbed a low talus, passed through a gap in the wall, and when out in the middle of what had been the orchard, I sat down. I felt myself at the center of my retreat, that I could go no further in any direction but within. And if necessary, I would disappear there, within, dis-appear altogether like a stone down a well into another kind of darkness. Then let it find me. Let it find me so far inside. Let it come as it would and be vexed by the hapless body I would leave behind. But then, I thought, what if it was al-ready there, within, waiting, had been, waiting, where only I could be, sharing my thoughts, watching my dreams? What ground could I take to clear it from my mind? What ground could I be certain of? Perhaps it was in my memory. Had become my memory. Had devoured my past to make me its own. I closed my eyes and listened to the quiet hollow of the dead grove. I could almost hear the hum of wasps, busy in the sweet pulp of fallen pears, and the rustle of brown and yellow leaves still clinging to the lowest boughs. I could al-most feel the warm air languishing in the fullness of the au-tumn season. Moments like these, brief as they were, assured me that there was still a kind of refuge to be found, a kind of home in the world stripped bare. But they were so easily lost, driven from me by the changing tempers of my mind. To hold them, to keep them where I could call them up at will, it was necessary to translate them into something solid, something lasting. Like the bright heartwood of a private language. Only there could I make myself a terrain as vivid as the earth's had been. Only there could I be the master of my making. This was the ground I was looking for. I picked up the bar I had carried out and cut back across the orchard toward the cloister. My mind was now full of ideas of what I might re-count, of how I might commence. But on the way back, a cold wind interrupted my thoughts with more immediate concerns. My feet were bare and I had only the blanket to cover me. In the dormitory were plenty of robes, woolen and warm. I would have two. And something for my feet. When light, I would collect my things from my room, look for some extra candles and food, and then decide what to do or where to go. The dormitory was off the upper gallery on the eastern side of the cloister. Access from below was gained by the night-stairs, which meant a trip back through the transept, back into its closed space and covered night. I struck the bar against a pillar and felt the pain ringing in my hand. I struck it again.

The door was just in front of me. I lifted the latch and gently eased it open. Darkness was all I should have seen, all I had hoped to see. I imagined the thickness of the gloom, everywhere and unbroken, even on the face of the far wall, where the faintest light would have shown. But something different met my sight, something I had clearly not expected. There was a fire. More than a fire. The church was in flames. My first thought was of the others and the fears they had had. Then I doubted the fact. I was tired. I was imagining. I shut my eyes, then looked again, but the draft now brought a blast of heat and smoke that drove me back. I closed the door, dropped the latch. Quickly, I would collect my things and get away, quickly collect my things and make for open spaces. My mind blank to any but that one purpose, blank but to collect my tins and food and bottles, I hurried out around the church, through the storehouse, and, once inside, toward my room. But there too, in the hallway leading down, it was stifling, the heat, and the fumes billowing not far behind. The flames were everywhere and out of nowhere and all at once. The gate, opening to the garden, I knew, I tried, but it too I found to be blocked, boards from somewhere having fallen. Boards fallen, simply fallen, I wondered, and the fire, from out of nowhere and everywhere, too much a thing too strange not to wonder, not to ask myself in an instant if there was something, the same thing, watching, working unseen. I doused myself with water from the fountain and circled, room to room, around the cloister, looking for an exit. But the windows were too small between the mullions. In the kitchen, in the guest rooms, in the workshops. All of them, the same. The cellar, I was hoping, would be different. I picked up a flaming spill that had fallen at my feet and hastened down into the long, low-ceilinged chamber below the almonry, into a strange atmosphere, of the earth, heavy, and cooler than above. But with my eyes slow to adjust and the torchlight too weak, I saw nothing for too long, saw nothing while the fire, not waiting, was raging overhead. And then, feeling as much as looking, going along the wall, torch up, I found a chute of some sort. I positioned a barrel beneath it and stuck the spill into the bunghole of another nearby. I climbed up and tossed the bar and blanket to the ground outside. Then I put my arms through, boosted myself with a kick, and drew myself out. In a moment I was standing on a gravel track in the western yard with the church on my right and the cloister behind me. How different it was outside, how the light shone, smoothly with soft shadows, reflected from the clouds of smoke like an eerie pall of false dawn. The flames, carried by the wind, had broken free from the buildings and were reaching across patches of barren rock, flitting and swirling, from tree to bush to tree. It seemed too peaceful a destruction, too warm and gentle a way to have it end, the stone upon stone, the sanctuary of so many for so long. As I walked on through the yard and down toward the valley over a series of broad flat stones, I felt more or less at ease, more or less as if the going were merely the telling of a story of some other time. I saw the words as blind, as tokens of belief, empty of end, empty of origin, but together building the illusions that carried me on through the streams of smoke. I felt untroubled by the flames that split the brittle cores of elms and cedars, undaunted as I listened to the whispers of the burning wood. Odd how it was all happening. Sparks from clumps of brush sprayed up in scintillant bouquets, and once their candescence had faded, the floating wisps filled the air like a snow of ash. But as if on a stage, as if the words were a place with nothing behind them, where everything, top to bottom, side to side, was language, where I was no closer to what I sought than to what I feared, where I had no contact, but had to continue, because I knew that without the words, or the place, I was nothing, that I was not something that could ever know the end of them. And so somewhere off the cloister a roof collapsed, and I thought not so much of what had happened as of the words I would choose to describe it. And this is how I watched the fire sweeping forward, outpacing me, rolling down to level ground and igniting the first of the many piles of timber left by the flood, and how I watched the flames lunging out and falling back as if to keep their balance among the loose branches and logs, and I considered how I would say, if I had to say, not that it was difficult, that another was alight, connected, I could only guess, by a trail of dry flood-wrack,

79

and then another and another, until there were too many to count, and then, I was down, off the slope, with the smoke coming in on all sides so thick that I could see nothing but what was before me, nothing familiar off anywhere, not the river, at any rate. And so I stopped beside a pool of water. And there I rested, but started to cough, and this was no good, I thought, as it got worse, and I knew I had to get out of there. So I wet my hair and soaked the blanket and set off wading into the channel that flowed from the pool. The sand, or was it mud, was firm beneath my feet and rippled in narrow ridges. The water was cold and black, but on its surface broke circles of light, spreading outward as I stepped. The piles were burning fiercely all around me. The timbers within were whistling. And the bright embers of bulky stumps were slipping silently down toward vanishing centers. I thought I saw faces, even, growing long in twisted ribbons of flame, so many faces burning, and bodies stretched out, piled to the sky. And I thought of the pyres of fallen warriors on some storied plain, dead because abandoned by their gods, surrounded by their legions, the living, standing, staying until dawn, when the carrion birds began to circle and the call came to move on, to move this mass of men onward, to leave what might be left, and make it easier for the others to forget. And winding, I went deeper, thinking now no orchard, no thickets of broom, thinking the old man ash under his stones, and winding, I went deeper, into the flames, blue now, burning blue, deeper into the warm curtain of their pure color, and thinking how the abbey, above it all, above the cities I had never seen, the distant lands I could only imagine, how the abbey would have been the last to go, and if what was last was gone, then there was nothing, nothing now to see, no place to be, and the earth, in the end, would be cold and sterile, like the white waste of a frozen star, cleared finally, to the last atom, of any hope of any chance of anything returning, and the fire burned on in still blue sheets, as if rising out of the ground, as if once loosened from the elements, it might desert the earth and soar through space bound for the sun, old source, and I noticed the blue growing paler, and wondered if my eyes, or if, no, if this was it, the end, paler, until, finally, nothing, no light, and I stopped and stood quite still and listened to myself breathe, but felt nothing cold, nothing of the earth dying, or how I thought it would be, and I tilted my head skyward, looking to see if I could see a last trace of light vanishing, light gone forever upward, but as I did, I sensed something different down below, something that hadn't been, and I bent to touch, and found no more stream, no more water, that I had stepped out, had left it, or it had left me, and what I touched was as soft as gray fox fur, and seen, now I saw, however faintly, a blanket of ash, and up above, no sky, no clouds, nothing but a white haze coming out of the darkness like a dense fog, only dry, and so much whiter, but tasting, oddly, not of smoke, no, tasting not of anything, or was it me, tasting nothing, smelling nothing, feeling nothing, not being, no, feeling something, the ground beneath my feet, and seeing still the whiteness gathering, so thick that I could see the gathering less and less, so close that it seemed a whiteness in my eyes or of my mind, and knowing something, knowing still that the words were coming, holding on to that, fixing myself on the silent voice, finding myself a constant cresting of its stream of words, to be conscious, happy to be conscious, to be thinking, not yet, not as long as I hear these words and feel this ground, not yet am I finished, though for the world itself little more could be said, looking as little like something as I could imagine anything being, dreamed as if by an old god, and gone as surely at his start, old god high in the heavens, and all vanished but the whiteness, the words, and the something beneath my feet, the whiteness falling, the words passing, time continuing, but beneath my feet everything was solid, there, at least, everything was solid, until I moved, left or right, backward or forward, in any direction, every direction, and then a sense, a seeming, of my ascending, while I moved, kept moving, and found myself rising, through the ash, soft to touch, rising, like the light had risen, rising into the brightness growing blue, and even bluer, sharper, until it was the sky I saw, the daylit sky, and feeling nothing of what I had felt before, ever before, nothing of the burden of my body, nothing of what had been and gone, feeling nothing but the light falling, and seeing high up on the stony mountains how it fell on slopes and shelves, and there, clinging like an outcrop of white quartz, was a city shining, a city seeming, of light itself, of nothing but the light

I am sitting on the steps of the square stone house where I sleep. It is clean and white like all the others, and like all the others, it is empty. The wind blows through the doors at will, but nothing else, apart from the light, comes or goes. At the end of the street the moon hangs over the roofs of houses like a slice of yellow rind.

The streets are narrow and straight, leading out from a central plaza of smooth white stones. At its center is a deep rectangular pool. When the wind dies in the late hours its water rests so still that stars appear on its surface as clearly as in the sky. There are no trees in the plaza, or along the streets, and it doesn't seem there ever were. There are no plants in the houses, no vines on the walls, no grass in the courtyards. There is no soil to speak of. Only the stones and the water and the wind and the sky.

Behind the house where I sleep is a terrace, and beyond the terrace is a precipice. When there are no clouds to block the view I often stand and look down to the valley of stone that lies in the distance below. The precipice only makes up one side of the city. The rest is surrounded by a wall of gray cliffs split by deep crevices. There are no gardens, there is no land. Only the stones and the water and the wind and the sky. And sometimes at night when I am lying quietly, I hear music like the movement of stars, once said to make small children smile in their sleep.

Yesterday I fell asleep in the afternoon sun and dreamt that I went up into the mountains. From the roof of a house I climbed onto the cliffs, and continued up, with little effort, through a steep field of gray scree toward the crest of the slope. The winds were wild about me, blowing in all directions. The glaring rays around the sun seemed frozen in the blue sky. I scaled one last row of boulders on the rim of the summit and crawled toward level ground. But when I looked up over the edge, I saw there was no ground. Only the quiet shallows of a wind-swept sea. I walked out among the waves until they hit me waist-high. Then I peered down to where a net of light played over a green mosaic of forms and saw I was standing in a bed of smooth round stones. I went under and lifted one out. I turned it over in my hands several times, thinking of another sea, soft and warm, where I had once been washed by waves of light. I put the stone back and walked further out. Shoulder-high, chin-high, until I was covered, until it was like walking along a corridor, but descending. Awareness now, of where I was, coming in blurred frames. One frame, steps. Another, stairway. Another, going down, down a long stairway. Down to a light at the bottom. Down to a life. As if I were a stranger long after my death, going down the steps leading down to those days. To the place where I had lived. To the street. The house. To the life I had lived and left behind.

Suppose I say he's not where he says he is, and that he's said he's there because there was no other way to say what I have to say. The fact is that none of this is quite the way he's said it is, but then I wouldn't say it was unfounded, wouldn't say it wasn't based on some measure of truth, some regard for accuracy. For example, it's true that this place is, in more than just a manner of speaking, the end of places, an asylum of extremity, hanging like a backdrop at the end of his world. It is true that he has come a long uncertain way enduring the doubt that attends every thought like a tiresome friend sitting at his shoulder. It is also true that after spending some time alone he found himself among a strange people and learned to speak their language. All these things are true. All these things and more. The abbey and the tannery. The endless rain. And in the course of all this, for it has its course, a significance of some sort has taken shape, unexpectedly, but surely, despite an inborn lack of faith in any saving grace. Presumption? Perhaps. But, that aside, we continue. Where truth fails opt for clarity. Avoid conclusions. To summarize: He set out from a place that had no beginning looking for a place where he might begin. He arrived at the place that is the end of places with no place left to go. Now the only way forward is to go back. All the way back. To begin again. In his own mind. Searching for his origins in wonder.

Deep in the memory of childhood remains a first inkling of divinity, on a night not darkening. Snowlit, like dusklight. He is lying on his back looking into the space below the ceiling, looking as if into a sky, and imagining himself on the brim of an eternal winter evening, when angels, like those of stories, descend from above, and he feels himself being lifted lightly, carried gently, upward, fearing from their realm no return.

Death comes later that winter. He stands in a dull rain watching her wave from a small window in a wall of brick. And then it's back to the old house to wait. A day or two or three. Wandering through its rooms full of carpets. Rooms beyond the reach of sunlight. The china cabinet. The curved glass. The key on a string. The snow falling on the sleeping village in the glass curio. Then hearing the words. From another room. Spoken in late night tones. I'm sure she recognized me. Tried so hard to talk. All I could do was guess at what she was saying. And hold her hand. At least she appeared comfortable. She was so frustrated earlier. Rosary and visitations in the evening. And then the body back to where the others are buried. Back to the small town in the middle of the endless plain. The journey by train. The arrival by night. And the day. The change from sunny and cold to sunny and warm. The green and white shoots spiking the garden. The first buds breaking into sunshine. Then the days growing longer, and the memory of that one, her last, growing shorter, moving deeper, into his mind.

The summer that will always be that season begins with afternoon storms and still evenings, swallows hurtling past the corners of the house and the shouts of children dying away into the aqueous nights. He sleeps beside an upstairs window open to the southern breeze and scent of osmanthus. The stars are brilliant in the sky more blue than black. He slips the latch on the screen to see them better. To see them as they are. As they move across the sky, and night by night through the seasons.

One morning several months later he leaves the warmth of woolen blankets, the flannel robe, the kitchen stove, and sets off beneath the streetlights. An hour till dawn. The grass is brittle beneath his feet. The church is empty. The lights are dim. He fills the cruets. Water and wine. Then makes his way down a narrow passage to the side chapel to light the candles. Alone for the moment. With the statues of saints. Their smooth eyes staring out.

At some point he noticed that everything had changed. The first buds. The swallows. The eyes staring out. The world had become a different place. He had become a different person. Wonder had become awareness. Still at an early age. Burdened with the pensum of presence. Not understanding what things were or why they were. Retreating into himself. But not quite knowing what that was either. At times he found it difficult to think that everything he was was there inside. And only there. Difficult to think that it was something only he could be. A body, yes, like any other. But with a voice and memory that no one else could know. A language. A world. Apart. Of dreams and lost days. No, it was not easy to understand, not easy to say why it seemed more real than anything else. And soon he found himself going further and further, going too far, and falling through whatever it was that held him where the others were. It became frightening, this falling, this disappearing so far inside. Down the same blind paths winding in and in upon themselves. To silken fields of pulsing surfaces, to dim hollows like chambers of hell. And it was the terror that one day he might not return which broke this habit as best it could be broken and got him to go back and be as close as he could be to what he had been before.

All of this has something to do with how he came to be in this place that is the end of places. Sitting at the top of his building at the edge of his city. The city of his pilgrimage. Sitting looking out over the terrace. Watching the crosswinds ferry white clouds through the sunlight. Despite the threat of rain. For the moment, at least, the clouds have parted and whitened against the blue sky like an apparition of heaven and the air is so pure it doesn't feel like air. And he is thinking, always thinking, searching for a way to bring himself out of himself, to return from awareness to wonder. But he knows that any attempt he might make will surely fail. If it's like any other plan he's ever had, he'll give it a little thought and then his mind will wander off to something else. His centrifugal mind. This has always been a problem. He'll be thinking about something—an idea, a thesis, a solution—thinking about, say, what direction his life has taken, will take, when he notices night has fallen and he begins to think of the darkness—how immense it is, or how it isn't anything, though when there is nothing, it is everything—as the muscles in his arms and legs drop off like so many snowbridges collapsing in the sun and his body begins to slip toward sleep, unless startled, as often happens, by some thought or another. Like how the beats of his heart have never stopped, can never stop. That they are to him all he will ever know of eternity. And he begins to listen too carefully, while each beat, coming with greater effort, stays each lapse longer, and he fears he may listen himself to death. But then a light comes over him, faint and formless, like candlelight through black linen, and he knows he is there again. In that unnamed place within himself. On that strange stage where he sees a life unknown outside itself. Drawn to this like an animal drawn to fire in the night. Drawn down to see what he is at the core, at the pounding furnace silenced by the softness of his body. Drawn like an animal to come too close, to see too much, and wanting all the while only to get out, away, to get somehow, somewhere, away.

I don't know how I can stay in this place. I don't know how I can stay in any place. Once I found peace in rooms. Rooms bright and unstinting in their stillness. Rooms well worth the space to drain the days. Rooms where nothing changed. Where time took nothing. Where only the past was present. But now I see that I have changed. That everything has changed. That time has taken me and all my memories. Moved us on toward that long dark night. Up among the high white walls.

But to get back to the story. To get back to it and get on with it. The only way I know how. He will be a young man. Like a photograph of what I was before I sat for too long. A fresh young face that ages in the space of its own reflection. Tired of thinking, considering, calculating, clarifying and confounding,

cracking his knuckles, and shredding his cuticles, he chooses
the alternative to the contemplative and goes down the many
flights of stairs in his building at the edge of his city at the
end of places to the street below. He leaves behind the para-
phernalia of his poverty: his papers, his pens, his books, his
table, his typewriter, his lamp, everything he would usually
have before him when he sits in his chair ready to begin. He
leaves behind the number of pages he has counted, the number of years it will take. He leaves all this behind. He puts
aside every idea of where he is going. And the very thought of
thinking about it he finds offensive. He stops when he reaches
the street and looks left, to the west, where the ring road
separates the city from a countryside of granite houses and
green fields. There is a gypsy camp in a grove of eucalyptus
trees to the north, and on a hill behind it, a school. A mile to
the south, down by the river, is a medieval abbey damaged
by fire and rebuilt as a state asylum. He looks to his right. It
is nearly midday, but the street, lying at the bottom of a chasm
of featureless buildings, remains in shadow. He pats his right
front pocket to make sure he has his keys, considers the tem-
perature, which he finds a little too warm, and then begins to
thread his way through the shifting crowds of people toward
a central plaza. It occurs to him how, at this hour, his city is
almost exclusively a city of women. Old women. Young women.
Middle-aged women. Mothers. Daughters. Widows in black.
Women. So many women. Most of them are carrying food,
parcels of fresh food for their midday meals. He is passed by
a woman in black balancing a staved milk-pail on her head,
by another bearing a basket of small green peppers, and by a
young woman with tawny skin and sun-sharpened eyes clutch-
ing a brown rabbit by the ears. Suddenly a shirtless boy approaches badgering him for money. Stepping to one side, he
digs down and comes up with a coin, but has to step, almost
stumble, over two old women sitting on the ground selling
squid from a gleaming bucket, sardines from a wooden tray.
As he presses back into the crowd, he feels a shower of lint
and dust and fluffs of hair falling lightly over his shoulders
and head, and looking up sees two arms and a rug vanish
into a window. A teenage girl in bright but ragged clothes

stops and shouts an oath. Her hand, sweeping through her dark bushy hair, brings a moth to light, which flutters away, climbing aimlessly toward the sky. Cool air is pouring from the open doors of apartment buildings and warm air is rising from the sewers. It is hot enough to make the summer currents that carry summer smells: tangy moldy smells, the smell of urine, the smell of fish, the smell of rotting fruit. Hot enough to vex the spirit with an assault of clamorous sounds: mechanical sounds of hammers and whirring cranes, of idling busses and trucks; human sounds of children crying, of vendors hawking. And all the while the idling busses and trucks are spewing gray and white and black smoke billowing, warping the air, toxic to his palate. At the corner he leaps a curbside torrent from a broken main and crosses behind an angry, impatient motorbike, and the jangling bed of a mason's van. Skirting the twig broom of a street-cleaner, he reaches the opposite curb. Here there are fewer people and he can see the sidewalk beneath his feet with its various signatures of life: the grease-stains of garbage, the excrement, the spittle, the orange peels, the peanut shells, the blood, the vomit, the coffee grounds, the broken glass. And as he is looking down he notices a change of light overhead. Clouds have appeared. He hears the flute of a knife-grinder calling for business, silverware clattering in a drawer, and a dog barking in an open window. He walks on. Every vacant shop he passes, every wall too long without vigilance is covered with layer upon layer of posters, torn and shredded by a host of passing hands to reveal a history of dead politicians, foreign theater groups, overweight singers, and oriental circuses. He is stopped by a gypsy woman with a baby carriage. She smiles a broad, gap-toothed smile and points to an infant monkey swaddled in a filthy blanket. She is smiling still as her level palm goes toward him. The tip of her middle finger touches his sternum and she utters something unintelligible. He smiles back, nods to her ward, and places a coin in her hand. He always enjoys walking the last fifty yards or so to the plaza. There is a slight incline, and the feeling of pushing himself a little harder, of stretching his legs that much more, he finds agreeable. But today, just as he reaches full stride, just as he enters the periphery of the plaza with all its movement and life, it begins to rain and he is forced to turn around and make his way back home, jostling with the people who have crowded beneath the narrow overhang of the buildings, jockeying for an inside track.

It is mid-afternoon and the rain has become a light mist. He has ventured out a second time, crossed the plaza, continued up the steep street directly to the north, walked along the cobbled avenue below the embankment lined with palm trees, climbed the stairs up to the park, passed through the corner known for its roses and toilets, entered the old part of the city at what was once the western gate, and sat at a table under a mossy awning to eat a flan and drink a cup of coffee. He has done all this and has finished. The flan was delicious. Since it is not the sort of day to sit out on a terrace and have a cup of coffee, he sits alone. Every now and then the waiter, wearing a white jacket and carrying a towel slung over his left forearm, comes and stands in the doorway, but he is not much company. The gulls, on the other hand, flying in low under the misting clouds, are. They come from the coast every morning to feast on the mounds of refuse gathered from the doorsteps of the city every night, and now they are on their way back. They break their lazy, irregular formations to wheel and backpedal, linger on a draft, long, undulant lines of them. By evening they will be passing over a small fishing village on the coast, then the brightly painted boats in its port, then the breakwater. By night they will have settled to roost on an island of rock and sand further out, along the rugged edge of the bay.

Think back to that first time you saw the sea. What fascinated you most was how the earth curved away beyond the horizon and left the eye nothing but an endless gulf of empty space to dwell on. In the evening the sunset was like none you'd ever seen. Not because of the colors, the greens and yellows and violets riding the waves, changing by the second. But because of the sense, the feeling of planet that you had never felt before, the feeling of a place that was of the stars, yet shimmering at your feet.

91

He pays for his coffee and flan, and dashes a few yards across the smooth granite pavement, slipping on a viscid film of mud, to the shelter of one of the arched passageways beneath the buildings of the old city. He hears an accordion and finds its player behind a column of gray and golden stone. The elderly man is playing a tango and twitches and bows his head in an ecstasy of tempo. He is wearing a visored cap pulled down on one side and his hollow cheeks are drawn to a tight, perhaps toothless, smile. Though he doesn't stop for anyone, a rakish twinkle in his eyes acknowledges those who stop for him. Further along a young woman is on her knees, hunched over a corner of the passageway. Her left arm is moving quickly in broad strokes, but her long brown hair hangs down nearly to the ground, concealing her hand, and it is not until he passes behind her that he sees she is drawing the radiant face of a religious figure on the cold dark stone. The shoebox beside her holds no money. Her chalk sticks, for the most part, are worn to stubs. He wonders where she sleeps, what she eats. She stops and turns to look at him. Her chin is on her shoulder. Her eyes are blue, icy blue. Her skin is white. His eyes move quickly to the drawing. He stands looking at it for a moment, then turns his body with a half step to signal his interest is concluding. With her thumb she tucks her hair behind her ear and flips what falls forward over her back. She turns to examine her work. He takes the opportunity to walk away.

You remember. It was a late summer evening. In the northern wilderness. On the upper story of that old house. The light refusing to die for what seemed like hours. Then bluish moonlight. Falling over the curves of her nose and chin and neck. Sculpting with shadow the desert contours of her body: her breasts and the bone of her hip rising from the sand-grain of her cool skin as if swept to their soft shapes by a night wind.

There are lateral arches and transverse arches. The transverse arches, which extend for approximately two and a half yards, rest, to the right, on graceless block piers. On the left, they send their thrust, or weight, down into the thick front walls of the shops along the arcade. The lateral arches, which separate the street from the passageway, share the same block piers with the transverse arches, but between these they come down on proper columns styled in a variety of orders from the simple to the composite, the latter bearing ornate capitals decorated with vines and animals of the native region. However, there are exceptions. In many cases the lateral arches go from block pier to block pier to block pier, rather than from block pier to column to block pier, and the block piers themselves are often masked with non-functional columns sculpted onto their sides. There is even a place where the building above rests directly on the block piers below with no arches at all. But he is not conscious of any of this as he goes down the passageway past two bookshops, a toy store, a pastry shop, a beauty salon, a row of silversmiths and a hat shop, nor does he notice the candlewax on the pavement from religious processions, nor the scallop shells carved on the walls and lintels, nor the coats of arms on several of the buildings that were once palaces. No, he is thinking about something else—the skeptical hypothesis of those famous meditations, the frightening theory that all of this is merely the deception of a malignant demon, or, to put it another way, that creation is in fact the wanton trick of a transcendent imagination. It is not a particularly apposite thing to be thinking, offering nothing to gain, nothing to lose. But nonetheless it is what has occupied his mind all the way down the street and what continues to occupy it up a gentle ascent past a bank, an umbrella shop, an appliance store, another toy store, and several gift shops. It occupies his mind as far as the end of the arcade, and there its occupation ceases, for just as he is stepping out from under the last arch, he collides with a small boy. The child's face is crimson and streaked with tears. His head is turning in all directions: He is lost. Without hesitating he opens the boy's fist, which has closed with panic, and takes his hand. Its grip is tight and automatic. The square where they are standing is empty and the mist is continuing to fall, so he leads the boy back under the arcade and explains that his mother is sure to find him if he stays in one place and waits for her. Then he tells him the story of another little boy who lost his mother once and walked all over the city looking for her only to find her in the very place where he thought he had lost her. He's not certain whether the boy has been listening to him, but his crying and shaking have largely stopped. The desired effect has been achieved. There are six ways of entering the square. One is from the south transept of the cathedral. One is from the adjacent square. And the remaining four are from narrow streets. He glances from one to the next trying to imagine what the boy's mother will look like. Five minutes pass and no one appears. The child's impatience is growing. To give him the feeling that something is being done, he takes him across the square and up a series of steps to continue their vigil in the doorway of the cathedral. A few pigeons settle on the fountain below. The bells in the tower above toll the quarter hour. Because of the rainy climate wildflowers of various colors sprout in thick clumps from the ledges and walls of the cathedral. He lifts the boy up over his head to harvest a few of these, and when they have a dripping bundle, he sets him down on his feet and proceeds to name each one for him. The vines with the tiny purple and white flowers are ivy-leaved toadflax, he tells him. The pink ones are red valerian, and the others are a purple sort of the same thing. The boy puts them to his nose, then offers them to his friend. Smell them, he says. He does. Fragrant. He nods. Very fragrant.

I'm sure you remember. Smell them one more time. Think back to that first summer. How you noticed them then. Think back to those first evenings spent sitting on the steps in the square to the east of the cathedral, when the sky was full of swallows and the air was cool in the long shadows. Impressed, you were so impressed by everything. For years you had wandered as if in a dream through that desert that had taken your mind. Until awakened. By the way the sunlight gilt the windows in the dome above the chancel. By the soft blending of music from different corners of the square. By what lay on the other side of the stones that surrounded you: the votaries in the convent behind the wall who dig a handful of earth

94

from their graves every morning before dawn, and the bones of the ancient lords and warriors buried beneath your feet in a kingdom of death older than history. But then the desert returned and the impressions disappeared like drops of rain falling on its sands. You went appropriating scenes and faces piecemeal without ever giving yourself over to their simple sense of being, without ever risking the boundary of your own flesh and blood. Until you came to the end. Until you could go no further. Until you thought you were dying, or blind at best, up there in your room, crawling over the barren mountains, through the cinders, fearing still your childhood sense of falling, falling too far inside, climbing out on words vanishing, certain all the while that in fact there was no relief to be found.

The bells in the tower above toll the half-hour. He has handed the boy over to a pair of policemen and has entered the cathedral by the door in the south transept. It is dark and, except for the drone of a few people praying, quiet. Behind the columns on the left is a table where tickets may be purchased to the cloister and museum. He approaches and puts down his money. A ticket is torn from the book and pushed across the table toward him. He picks it up, folds it, and slips it into his shirt pocket. He goes out the door and starts down the eastern walk to his left. The ground is covered with the graves of noblemen and he can feel the keys and towers and boars and stars of the crests that adorn them through the soles of his shoes. It is the long way around and he goes unhurried. There are imposts on each pier, and on each impost rests a half column, whose ribwork, as it rises, fans out into delicate rays of stone, which, crossing each other, make elegant webs, forms of perfection, to support the vault above. Perfection. No other word will do. The cathedral, unlike the street, is a closed world of perfection. Each side of the cloister mirrors the other. Two piers, an opening. Two piers, a corner. Two piers, an opening. Two piers, a corner. The symmetry is so perfect he can almost see himself watching himself as he passes in the opposite direction on the opposite side. And as he starts a second lap he wonders of the others who have walked the circuit of this cloister, of the person who walked it more than any other, walked it at night, walked it at dawn, and if another, walking it in the sun, walking it in the rain, ever wondered who might come and wonder at his countless revolutions, and if yet another might someday wonder as he is wondering of the others, if he himself ever wondered of the others who would one day come, and he can almost see that person passing in the future, on the opposite side, in the opposite direction, by the openings, by the piers, see that person passing, watching, wondering. And as he starts a third lap the man at the table where he bought his ticket comes out to see what he is doing. He slows his pace, clasps his hands behind his back, hangs his head a bit, and puts on the countenance of one who is deep in meditation. When he reaches the northwest corner of the cloister he takes the expected route into the dark hallway and goes up the stairs past the worn tapestries of hunters and rustic cottages and peasants drawing water from a well, past the statue of the saint in the niche, all the way up to the door of the museum. But instead of entering, he turns to the right and goes out onto the balcony. He continues down its length before stopping in the far corner to lean against the railing. The mist has let up and the clouds have risen a little. On the distant horizon he can see a blue band of sky, and after a moment or two, he can see sunlight shining on the ridge of mountains that stands between himself and the sea.

He spends the rest of the afternoon, the evening, and part of the night walking the streets. He wants to take in every detail of everything he sees because he knows it will be the last time he will see any of it again. He goes slowly, describing each scene to himself in his own way in order to remember it better. By dusk he has been up and down the four principal streets of the old city and through most of the alleyways that comprise its northern quarter. But his desire to walk is unabated. He follows the avenues and lanes that curve around the city where its walls once stood and searches out every cul-de-sac and passage he may have missed before. There are fewer people on the streets with each hour that goes by and he begins to notice those who have already crossed his path once or twice. There is an old man with matted hair talking to himself in a foreign language. There is a young man wearing a torn corduroy suit blackened with grime. There is a look about these people that tells him they walk the streets every night, walk them endlessly. As he approaches the square at the southern end of the street where he came across the accordion player, he can hear the hydraulic groaning of sanitation trucks. Their presence near the terraces of the cafes causes the customers to pay and go. The waiters come out, exchange a few friendly words with the drivers, and leisurely stack their chairs and tables. He asks one of them the time. It is nearing two o'clock. He decides to circle the old city once more, and starts out down a narrow street of sawdust bars and restaurants, turning eastward at the cathedral, and advancing uphill past a large monastery before passing through a modest plaza and coming into the market where he stops momentarily to watch the maintenance crews hosing damaged fruit, flowers, and animal matter from the stones to prepare for another day. When he begins again, it is in the direction of home. His return takes him back past the cluster of cafes, back through the corner of the park, back along the avenue lined with palms, back across the central plaza, and back down his street to his building, where he climbs the one hundred and twenty-four steps to his door. He proceeds directly to the terrace where he drops into a deck chair, rests his arms at his sides, and breathes in the scent of roses and gardenias. The clouds above are sheer and light like cotton wool stretched thin, and the stars are visible, plainly visible, shining through.

He sleeps soundly until early afternoon when he wakes beneath slow-moving clouds, cumulus, covering the sun. He lies there a while half-mesmerized as they float lazily by. Under such a sky it is easy to imagine himself leaving that place, stealing away on an ordinary afternoon, disappearing like a dark dream from the light of day, into the pleasure of a world without him.

The first large box he takes down to the curb is full of clothes. The second contains his photographs, books and papers. The third, his plates and cutlery, curtains and towels, two lamps and a broken iron. On his last trip upstairs he waters the flowers on the terrace, looks around his room one more time, and walks out without so much as bothering to shut the door. Back on the street he sees that the boxes have been emptied. He crosses the street at the corner and follows the ring road north to the top of the hill. At the next corner he cuts northwest through the university campus, then north again until he comes to a dusty park at the end of a long street that begins at the foot of the cathedral. The area is more rural than urban with open fields behind the houses and the street deteriorating into a rough lane of broken tiles and chipped stone. But as it winds down along the wall of a large estate the rubble thins and he can tell by the smooth regular stones that it was once a well-traveled route. Soon another wall curves around from the north to face that of the estate, and the two of them, together with the tangles of ivy and tufts of purple flowers that cover the stones, form a close, almost stifling passageway. Biting clegs circle around him and lizards move in the nettles and spearmint that crowd the path. The stream below lies at the bottom of a deep ravine and because of this its smell, that of human settlement, precedes every other intimation of its presence. When he reaches the ancient, triple-arched bridge he looks down over the side to the lush green banks that drop vertically into shadow and vent a summer spiciness, which irritates his nose and eyes. He stands there a moment, then crosses to lean over the other side. His first thought when he looks downstream and sees the tannery is that it is not at all as he has remembered it. Along its northernmost wall is a garden of sunflowers, gourds, corn, and kale watered by the seepage from two parallel channels that come down from upstream and disappear into the foundations of the works. The roof has long since gone. Not a single beam remains to rot and nourish a single fern. Cascades of ivy, blossoming honeysuckle, and hedge bindweed bury the walls upon whose upper surfaces stand stalks of fennel three feet high. He walks around to the western side of the ruins where a small reservoir has been converted into a washing basin and clusters of brambles are hung with drying clothes. The two doors he remembers have been bricked up so he looks through a window rendered impassable by rusty iron bars. The pits are mostly covered with creeping vines and dark green ferns. A small bay laurel stands rooted in one. He counts the number of years that have passed since that morning when he discovered what had happened. He must have walked miles that day, up and down the streets, until he came to this place. It was the quietest he could find. Though close to the city, it seemed like something out of another world. He notices the bees hovering, searching, over the brambles' white flowers and the sparrows chattering, skirmishing, as they fly from wall to wall. Better not to think about it, he tells himself, as he turns and steps carefully through the watercress and back along the walkway to the path. On the slope to the west are the stables where the animals were kept and slaughtered. He passes them and continues up into an open field of grass and wildflowers swarming with flies and bees, then reaches the summit of a small knoll after a short ascent and faces east to look at the city one more time. It is evening now and the towers of the cathedral are a pale orange against the lavender of the haze behind them. He sees a flock of white birds over the old part of the city catch the sunlight at some point in their circling, then lose it in a turn and disappear, then catch it again, then lose it again, like louvers opening and closing in the fading sky. It is hard for him to believe he is looking at it for the last time. This place that has been his life for so long. He turns away and walks down into a pine forest that spreads westward from the hill. It is a steep descent at first over the rutted stones of a cart-path, and he goes slowly, almost respectfully, hoping not to disturb the quiet that surrounds him. Long shafts of sunlight lance the gloom beneath the forest ceiling and break into pools of molten color on the sloping ground. A crow calls out to warn of his approach and a thrush can be heard moving through the dead leaves in a covert of brambles and alder buckthorn. He stops for a moment to fashion a staff from a fallen sapling, trimming its branches with a sharp stone, and then continues on his course. In a clearing a little further along where the ground begins to level off, he finds an old woman standing alone with a cow. Like every other woman her age, she is wearing nothing that is not black: black shoes, black stockings, a black dress, a black sweater, and, despite the warmth of the evening, a black overcoat, fastened at the top with a single black button. The coat is worn over her shoulders like a cape, hiding her arms. From one side emerges a walking stick, from the other a rope that is looped over the neck of the cow. As he passes, the animal raises its head and flicks it tail at the mud on its flanks, but the woman is as still as a statue, and does not respond when he nods. From the light of the clearing he returns to the darkness of the woods. The pines give way to a variety of trees along the banks of a small stream that comes tumbling down from higher ground. He crosses it on a row of slippery stones and once on the other side bends to wash his face and drink from his cupped hands. A blackbird begins to sing somewhere among the branches of a beech in the shadows of the opposite bank. The air is completely still and the haze has thickened. He stands, stretches his arms and legs, and sets out again on his way, climbing yet another incline. This part of the path is strung with scores of taut webs whose colorful spiders are fat with summer feasting. The strands are strong enough to endure his taking them down and re-hanging them in order to pass, until the light begins to falter and he is forced to swing his stick before him to keep from being entangled. The track continues to rise, but he can see nothing of the valley below or guess how far up he has come. When he finally reaches what seems to be the top of the ridge, night has fallen. He leaves the path in search of shelter among the granite boulders that stand like sentinels in the starlit haze, guarding the gorse and stunted pines of the exposed terrain. Feeling his way gingerly through the prickly scrub, he flushes a startled bird from its nest and stops to listen to the whirr of its wings diminishing quickly into the darkness. As he continues he hears others rustling uneasily in the undergrowth, and then the bark of a dog echoing up the valley from a village below. After wandering up and down through the dense brush for longer than he would like without finding any adequate cover, he sits on the edge of a large rock overlooking a steep drop to the northwest. A few lights flicker from a group of houses in the valley. The dog barks again and is silent. A gentle breeze carrying the scent of woodsmoke blows across his face. He climbs off the rock, walks down the slope a little, and enters a grove of short thick pines. It is dark inside, darker than the night, and to avoid the sharp ends of unseen branches he must bend low. The ground is covered by a deep layer of dry needles and is as soft as a down cushion. He lies on his back, clasps his hands behind his head, and in a matter of minutes is fast asleep.

That night he dreams of a sea within a dream, the sun-warmed surface of a restless sea, where he sits wrapped in a sheet of oilcloth watching the foam break from the bow of a wherry, filled with joy at the flying spray, at the taste of salt on his tongue, at the sting in his eyes, as the small boat rises and falls over the rolling waves, making its way through the outer rocks, moving steadily toward the island, but dreaming within a dream, he wakens within a dream, wakens to find himself lying in the dark listening to a thunderous sea and the raging gales that drive it, to mounting breakers surging across the salt-marsh, spreading to cover the garden plots that skirt its changing shore, but wakens too to hear a muted sound below the roar, the sound of softly splintering wood, the subtle encroachment of creeping waters, seeping through the floorboards quietly, gradually, in scattered wells, as if calmed by the stillness of the house, and hears the slow, al-most imperceptible collapse of walls as he is lifted up and carried out over black waves to the far side of night to make landfall on a faint shoreline in the amber light of coming day, an island coast of clean white sand and marram grass, where wine-colored clouds hang above the horizon in a gloom of sea-haze and the dawn lingers as the wind rises and the pale moon sets.

Then comes a flash of blue light. Then a tremulous clap of thunder. He wakens. This time to no dream. This time the rain is pouring through his pine enclosure and blasts of wind are riffling the branches from overhead. He rises to his feet. Water is trickling through his hair and running down his neck under the collar of his shirt. There is another flash followed instantly by a loud crack and a long low rumble. He wonders whether to leave or stay, whether he can make it down to the village or not. Close by the bough of a tree snaps and falls to the ground. He crouches down and crawls to the edge of the grove. The rain is coming in horizontally along with wind-borne scraps of leaves and twigs. A skein of lightning laces the sky and he can see enough of the hillside to know that the descent will not be easy, but he has decided it is necessary. He dashes out and over a fallen tree, tearing through the gorse with his head and shoulders turned away from the wind. The rain penetrates to his skin in a matter of seconds and is coming down so heavily that he must blink constantly to keep his sight clear. The ground is saturated and in a patch of spongy peat he loses his footing and falls. As he pulls himself up he sees a strange green luminescence in the sky, like the glow of the night sea, revealing the velocity of the clouds on their broken march eastward. Covered with mud, short of breath, and struggling to keep his balance, he carries on running, guided more by the grade of the terrain than any sense of direction. Lightning strikes a tree on the ridge above sending out a shower of sparks and a jarring boom. He slides down an embankment of slick leaves and manages to avoid stumbling headlong by breaking his fall against a tree. In this fashion, moving from tree to tree, he hastens down the steepest part of the slope until he is forced through a corridor between two large boulders where he discovers a path that leads to a lane which winds past fields of corn and hay and finally enters the village from its upland side. The windows of the houses are shuttered. There is no point in knocking. He considers a dovecote, but decides against it. Instead he climbs up into a corncrib that stands three or four feet above the ground on granite stilts. The wind is streaming in through the slats of its sides, but only a light mist from the rain is able to enter, and he assures himself that at this distance he can slip away once morning comes without being discovered by the inhabitants of the village. He is wrong.

Sleeping deeply, contentedly, undreaming, untroubled, he feels a ray of bright sunlight fall across his face and hears a woman's voice cry out. He opens his eyes, sees the door of his shelter hanging slightly ajar and quickly throws his legs out and jumps to the ground. Three men, wearing black jackets, dark trousers, and black berets are walking toward him. One is carrying a shovel. An old woman, plodding through the mud in her short heavy boots, circles around from behind and gives him a push as if to direct him toward the nearest house. When he doesn't respond she jabs him in the small of his back with the butt end of a scythe. This time to some effect. The men stand to one side to let the two of them pass and then fall in and follow behind. An emaciated dog brings up the rear of this procession that is soon joined by a pair of women who have been working to drain a garden ditch.

The house is a two-story block of unpainted cement embossed with orange lichens and stained here and there with a fur of brown fungus. Its pantiled roof, weathered gray and brown, is held in place by a scant provision of small field-stones. Chickens are shooed from the doorway as the party passes over the threshold and into a large front room. There is a bar on the left where two bottles of wine stand on a long smooth board polished by the elbows and palms of working people. On the right is a shop where canvas shoes and plastic buckets and boxes of detergent are piled on a countertop. A chair is picked up and put in the middle of the room.

"Sit down."

From a bare light bulb over his head a spiral strip of flypaper hangs, covered with flies. A middle-aged woman comes in from the kitchen drying her hands on her apron. She is the only person present not dressed in black. A moment later two children, a boy and a girl, race in and clamber up onto the counter where they sit and swing their feet.

"Maybe we should call the civil guard."

"Bah! The civil guard."

"He probably just got lost in the storm."

Three more people appear in the doorway.

"Can you understand?" The old woman shouts.

"Yes," he says.

She turns around to the others and smiles.

"Are you hungry?"

103

"Yes."

With a labored gait she walks over to the bar, steps up on a stool and cuts down a stick of salami hanging from the ceiling. She slices several pieces of it onto a plate, shakes out a dozen crackers from a box, walks back across the room and deposits the lot in his lap with an air of indifference.

"Eat."

"Thank you."

He can feel their eyes on him as he proceeds, and fixes his own on the floor until the dog comes around and stands directly before him. He gives it his last cracker.

"What would you like to drink, water or wine?"

"Wine, please."

One of the men hands him a glass and fills it. The woman takes his plate. He drinks.

"You're not from around here."

"No."

"What are you doing here?"

"I'm walking to the coast."

"The coast. Well."

"Is it far?"

"Walking? A day. Two days. Maybe three. Depends."

"On what?"

"On how fast you walk."

A ripple of laughter spreads around the room. Then a child asks, "What did he do?"

"Nothing."

Somewhere in the valley a series of fireworks explodes. The dog raises its ears. The children scramble off the counter and push their way past the people standing in the door. One of the men is rolling a cigarette.

"You'll want to cross the stream at the bridge and take the path leading north," he says.

"North?" says another.

"Over the bridge."

"Not to the coast."

"That's the way we always went."

"Not to the coast."

"North."

"You cross at the water mill and go up the hill. That's west."
"I never did. That's the long way around."
"That's straight. That's west."

The man smoking spits a flake of tobacco from the tip of his tongue and shakes his head. He draws deeply on the cigarette and turns to blow the smoke outside. His partner in the discussion is rolling one of his own and steps down to the yard before cupping his hands and lighting it. Seeing that there is nothing more to be discovered, the people that remain file out one by one with an automatic word of parting. The middle-aged woman wipes the bar with a wet cloth, corks the two bottles and retires to the kitchen. She is followed by the older woman who stops a moment to adjust her scarf and then turns to say "I'll have water put in the barn. You can wash yourself there. Today is a feast day. We'll be going over to the next village."

The hollow reports of distant fireworks and mortars continue to roll across the valley calling people to the festival. A small column of villagers passes beneath a row of white poplars that sway and shiver in the fresh breeze. The stream they follow creases the green fields of its narrow plain as it rushes eastward falling at intervals over defiant bedrock until after a mile or so it slips through a mossy gorge, slows a little and meets its twin fork from the north. But they do not follow it this far. Taking their leave before the end of the mile, they turn north and climb through a treeless maze of rundale plots whose walls have fallen and whose vital earth will yield nothing more than an early autumn harvest of blackberries for the birds. When they reach the crest of the ridge that slopes down to the confluence of the two streams a small settlement comes into view. There are twenty or thirty houses huddled together and a church with two belfries higher up on the right. A festive mixture of music, amplified voices, fireworks, bells and the buzz of human intercourse drifts on the breeze with varying strength to reach their ears. As they step down over the stones of the footpath and help each other across runlets spawned by the storm, others like them, tenants of hidden villages on rocky hillsides or in valleys no less remote, are following similar paths, listening to the same sounds, looking forward to the feast of their local saint and the celebration of midsummer.

He feels his eyes begin to water from the blue smoke that hangs under the tarpaulin where he has seated himself at a rough table with his hosts for something to eat. First come white bowls that are filled to overflowing with a heavy purple wine from a white pitcher, then comes a large round loaf of warm bread sliced in wedges, then wooden plates of squid and octopus dripping an oily yellow sauce. He picks at these rations scrutinizing those parts of the dead creatures that still distinguish them, and drinks his wine. He finishes his second bowl as a woman tells him about her son who was lost at sea, and then excuses himself and steps outside. The narrow concourse is thronged with people. Stalls have been set up under umbrellas or sheets of canvas on either side of the corridor where vendors are selling everything from footballs and clothes to cheese and bread to aniseed pastries skewered on sticks. He lets himself move with the crowd past a man with a microphone peddling funeral wreaths and silver polish, past a booth where music blares above a table piled with tapes, past a boy straddling a bicycle whose merchandise, including postcards, flags, earrings, shawls and towels, hangs pinned to his coat. At the end of the lane a sharper shifts his cards on a fruit crate while several wary onlookers watch his hands. Behind them a flock of sparrows drops from a sprawling oak to search for food in the deep grass. As he turns to retrace his steps a blind woman seated on a stone bench before a house calls out: "You haven't far to go." He slips into the crowd without looking back and, pushing and shoving as vigorously as he is pushed and shoved, sets off toward the church. Though the stairs leading up to it are less than fifty yards away, it takes him the better part of ten minutes to cover the distance. There are beggars on every step: mothers and grandmothers holding out the scarred or crippled limbs of their children, a one-legged gypsy resting his stump on the lower rung of a crutch, a white-haired man with a subnormal boy holding his hat in his hands as he gazes at the ground. Other children stand and stare with curiosity from beyond the baskets of coins that sit on the ground surrounding the mendicants. He climbs to the top of the stairs and presses into the churchyard past a woman doing penance on her knees. Somewhere in the crowd someone is moaning. It is a primitive sound, almost animal, but evokes no reaction from those around him. He turns his body and sidles forward using his shoulder to create openings where none exist, pushing past elbows, rubbing up against busts and bellies, mixing his sweat with the sweat of others, to move closer to the church. Someone else starts to moan behind him and he can sense something in the air. The crowd shifts and he is pushed aside by the crush, pressed between someone's back and someone's chest. His forearms are drawn up close to his body and when he cannot free them he feels his heart jump and a panic in his breath. The murmur of conversation suddenly drops off. A heightened expectancy charges the atmosphere. People are on their toes. He turns and sees a woman to his right collapse into a trance, writhing in a silent fury, as though consumed from within by fire. Two men take her by the arms as her body, able to twist no tighter, lurches forward, grotesquely arched and taut to the point of breaking. From out of the church, standing on a palanquin, borne on the shoulders of the penitent, comes an icon wrapped in blue velvet and crowned with a diadem of precious stones. It moves into the crowd, swaying from side to side, seeming to cut down those that stand in its path, staring blankly through its glassy eyes, an object so unreal, a tiny queen of sylphs, a still-born child stuffed and painted, an avatar from beyond the deepest blue of heaven. As it advances toward the woman, sending a swath of humanity before it, she starts to rant and roll her head, digging in and pushing back, straining every sinew, until it reaches her and she freezes, her teeth clenched, her eyes transfixed. It passes over her quickly, quietly, pitching like a buoy in restless waters, and she is lifted unconscious, or cured, or dead by trembling hands from the dark currents of its wake.

That evening he joins his hosts beneath the grape arbor behind their house. Because it is a festival day there are fresh sardines broiled on an open fire and a side of goat flavored with clove and parsley. The meal lasts several hours, lengthened considerably by coffee and brandy and the strawberries they pick for dessert as they walk through the garden in the long summer twilight. He is taken to one side by the old woman, great-grandmother, as she is called, and told of the pilgrims' way westward leading to the sacred mountain at the edge of the sea. You must follow the large stone crosses, she advises him, starting just upstream beyond the granary. The men soon wander off to smoke cigarettes in the darkness, leaving the women to put away the food and wash the dishes. The table, a slab of cement set on a nether millstone, is cleared and covered with a soft, musty pallet to become his bed. The children come out to wish him good night, and then, at last, he finds himself alone. He lies down in his clothes and gazes at the dark underside of the arbor, at first wondering, but then dreaming of those occasions when the wine from its clusters of swelling grapes will be drunk, of the christenings and burials, the weddings and festivals, and the other days, the ordinary days, remembered briefly if at all, when a barn is built, when the fields are plowed and the grain is sown, when the corn is spread on a stone to dry and the briar and bracken are burned from the roadside, ordinary days that pass in a timeless procession as the year moves down the far side of its cycle, dying with the smell of pine smoke and the rainy autumn mornings and the quiet moment spent beside an iron stove on a gray afternoon braiding the flaxen hair of a blue-eyed child. The dog snaps at a moth just outside the kitchen window. When the light goes off it pads around for a few minutes, scratches at the door, and then curls up under the table with a contented yawn and click of its teeth.

He opens his eyes without being aware that they have been closed. It is still dark out. He eases himself up onto his elbows and takes a moment to collect his thoughts, to remember where he is and what he's doing, then slips off the table and walks softly across the terrace to a cistern where he splashes water on his face and wipes the sleep from his eyes. A rooster crows. The dog stands and stretches. The pigs, roused, shift and thump the side of their shed. He looks around instinctively, thinking there is something, something he should, but no, there is nothing. The fragrance of privet sweetens the night air that cools his skin as it dries. He walks down to the bottom of the garden, climbs over a wall buried beneath a mass of eglantine, and follows the track up past the granary to a large stone cross where he takes off his shoes and socks and steps into the shallows of the stream. Its water is cold and heavy, pulling at his legs like the pure sediment of night's gravity, pulling powerfully, as if inviting him down. Deliberation slows his going as he attends the sleek streamworn stones underfoot and the waterweeds slippery between his toes. A moment later he emerges, sits and picks the clinging strands from his legs, slaps his feet and rubs them dry. Whispers of a breeze stir among the treetops. He stands, calced and ready, surveys the slope before him and begins to climb. The path is an ancient road that shifts at sharp angles from left to right and right to left over windstripped, rainslashed ledges and sheets of stone. Spring water trickles under the rocks and a solitary owl calls out from its invisible perch among the pines. As he approaches the dark ridge above raised steeply against the stars, it gives way to another further on, which, as he climbs higher, gives way to yet another, a final summit moving elusively out of reach, rolling back into the distance, higher into the sky. Sight of the village in the valley below has been lost and he sees instead stars floating beneath him on the lowland haze. Stars beneath him. Stars above him. He feels himself among them. The swan and lyre, the gorgon-slayer, the seven sisters sailing, and falling forward through the night like a satin scarf is the stream of light that leads him westward on his way, as near to him now as it was to the others who came before and built this path pursuing the end of their horizons, some limit lying beyond their lives. He reaches a pass and a second cross. To the north a soft white cloudbank blooms in boreal winds to presage dawn. By coming this way in life these people sought to hasten the journey after death, to ease their passage to the world beyond the outer fringe of places. It is a path that the living and the dead travel together, a realm where neither is certain, and both are blessed and damned with an awareness of the other seen or heard, somehow always known. To him the other comes as a voice, lightly blown across the bending grasses, carried more like a presence than a sound, recognized at once as his own, calling to him from among the dark steles and cenotaphs of stone, the voice of himself as a child, calling to him from its other world. How he could be there and here, then and now he does not know, but fears how little distance lies between them, fears that in this place, among the tenebrous peaks and flickering stars, he might slip too easily from his body and be blown by the roving winds too far to return. On his right, overlooking a deep gorge, is a large mound, a tumulus perhaps, or fort, crowned with a ring of stones. A narrow path takes him down across the damp ground of what was once a moat or reservoir and then up along the rim of a rounded embankment. The stones of the outer wall lie dispersed in a wide band, pushed aside by the gorse, undermined by heavy rains. He shelters himself on the lee side of a large rock at the center of this circle. The stars have already begun to fade, and the eastern sky, lit like a vast stage in the night, is soon shining a radiant shell pink. Piercing cries overhead alert him to the hovering silhouettes of a half dozen kestrels braced against the solid face of a steady wind. He leans back to see them better, but feels a sharp pain in the palm of his hand. It is the skull of a viper. One of many that lead him to find coils of bleached bones scattered on the ground in loosely gathered rags of rotting skin, and on the boulder behind him, crevices full of tiny white hoops and splinters caked with streaks of guano and matted wisps of down. The first rays of morning light soon reach the burrows and granite hollows of the mound, and the earth itself seems warmed to life, as slow and sinuous bodies slide out over each other, tasting the air and slipping from sight. He begins to retreat very cautiously, collecting a handful of stones and throwing them at anything that moves, afraid to bend and pick up more though pausing every few feet until he reaches the embankment where the steep clear slope reveals a return to uninfested ground. Then, cutting back through deep clumps of gorse, tramping blindly as the swinging branches draw beaded lines of blood across his face and arms, he edges up to a gap that opens out to the path and yet another cross where he sits a moment to catch his breath. The wind has died away and there has come a softness to this summer morning, a clemency of blue bearing upon scents of earth and air, upon distant sounds, a feeling of return, of life full beyond the memory of days. The sea cannot be far, and the island and the deep wet grass and the misty dawn rising slowly as it has risen so many times before, and he sets off again as he has in dreams, as if in lives, down the path. For the rest of the morning he follows its winding course over the contours of the upland ridge through undulating fields of wild grasses and bell heather, past great piles of granite boulders to stark promontories where he hopes for a first glimpse of sunlight shimmering off the moving surface of the open sea. But he comes down each time more disappointed than before, having beheld to the north and south, beyond the breach of valleys, only the far horizons of lonely moors, and to the west repeated vistas of rocky elevations breasted by pine groves and the low ragged profile of heath and scrub. In a saddle between two such elevations, at its center, where the rain collects to form a spongy, brackish mire, the path becomes a maze of ruts scattered by hassocks of turf and hidden stones. A track emerges at the far end of the hollow, but curves down toward the valley to the south. The ancient road must lie somewhere to the north of this, preserved if forgotten, and he searches the sedge and shallow pools until he finds it, divining before seeing its slight impression, a wide wrinkle in a carpet of red and white clover leading him up over rising ground in a westerly direction. This divining serves as prelude to a growing feeling of familiarity, a bewildering sense of seeing things again, of recognizing everything from the shapes of hills to the signatures of noon shadows. Perhaps it is a symptom of his isolation. Perhaps not. He is led by this sense, this uncanny certainty, to a field of kale thriving where it could not be, cleaving to the granite earth, and on to a stone house behind this field surrounded by a blaze of fuchsia, where he finds sitting on a stone bench a woman older than he would know her, plying straw with thick red

111

fingers, plaiting it, plying it, molding it, trimming it. He approaches and she stops. With rapid passes her blind eyes seem to search for his face. She asks, "Do you know who I am? Do you remember me?"

"You called to me at the festival."

"At the festival, yes. At the festival. But not before, no, you do not recognize me from before, you who would be young again with the eyes that cannot see. Come with me."

She reaches for his hand and leads him across a country lawn of small white daisies, through a cemetery where the stones are carved with ghostly whirlwind characters, past a chapel, to a spring. Deep among the ferns she invites him to drink the clear cool water, and as he does he feels the dark shadow of his presence somehow cleansed, seeing for the first time the transparence of himself, his memories, dreams and desires as patterns woven like the paths of bees seized to dance in a color-foraging kingdom of wildflowers. He rises from the liquid braid. The woman speaks.

"You haven't far to go," she says. "You must follow the sun as it falls, fix your sight and follow it falling, over these fields bringing saffron to life from new buds breaking scent from deep roots as earth sugars surge for flowers to flower again. Follow it over the stones of this path, the silent barrows figured with the glyphs of man, over the mountain peaks at twilight, under the evening star, vailing behind the fells when the light is gathered in the colors of the rainbow at the earth's dark edge. Let me show you the way."

She takes him up to a rocky mount where they stand beside the statue of a saint with a set of keys. From there at last he sees what he has waited so long to see, the sacred mountain rising above the valley haze, its peaks like spires blue before the shining plane of water seeming to tilt up toward the sky behind it. And across the bay, like a half-submerged leviathan crouching on its haunches, lies the final headland beyond which there is nothing. The woman touches his arm and then turns and walks away without another word. He climbs down over the rocks into a blue valley where the heather is just coming out and the broom is almost past and the full-blossomed boughs of the elder trees are listing in the honeyed light. Massive stones set one atop another form the spare fragments of the plundered tombs of kings and warriors who came this way to find the end that found them first. The engraved outlines of halberds and daggers, the cupmarks and calendric spirals testify in a distillation of terms to the content of their lives. Rooks circle warily among the tallest pines while dunnocks flit and scatter among hedges of briar and dry-stone walls. He leaves the path, cutting through idle terrain, making his way toward a lower peak, thinking how geographies gain things, engrain them for him, keep him from his own absence closing in behind him, and he sees himself as a kind of spirit moving down the slope, creating a course like a thought through the mind of the world; every move is a decision made, every act an art, his going as eloquent as any group of words. The sun edges behind the mountain and evening shadows begin to rise from the depths of the valley. He crosses a bridge of stone slabs set on stone piers dressed in bright green moss. Crepuscular hawks have taken to the sky and a light breeze falling from the cooling heights brings him his first taste of the sea's salt air. Then he climbs, climbs as so often, through the pines, through the gorse, conscious in his presence of an end more palpable than the darkness encroaching. Above the forest on a grassy ledge below the summit of this peak a life lived alone among the ghosts of pink granite survives itself in a refuse of bones, of shells and shards of pottery, and footholds cut in a solid face of rock that lead him up to a narrow platform of wind-carved cauldrons and crude foundations, up as high as the very top where he finds a rough inscription reddened by a dry alga reading

X . REGES : EPs . PRs OMN
IBvS . DE DEO : EXCOMVN I
CAVERVNT : IPsvM : CASTELLvM

For an indeterminate length of time he sits looking into the light, the late evening light, losing himself to a state where moments fall away without sequence, fleeing the fixtures of his mind, like the sky fading and the day passing from amethyst to indigo. Nightbirds call out in the stillness. Streetlamps like strings of pearls blink on in the quiet ports below and a lone beacon on the headland begins its sweep through the sea-haze, flashing at intervals off the running surface of the evening tide. He descends slowly, precariously, down the far side of the rock, searching, straining for fissures or shelves to support his weight until he eases himself onto a ridge, sharp and serrated, that reaches out across the darkness to the pale dome of the high massif. Summoning his weary arms and legs to the effort yet again, he crawls along clasping the smooth warm stones as currents of hot and cold air stream around him. Stars appear in the sky, and in the villages far below, deep in the mountain folds, solstice fires burn like their reflections. Fires far out on the horizon he remembers and the smoke drifting toward the stars, and the songs—those songs so markedly incantatory, come back to him as more than a memory, and the voice too, that voice, of a single child, singing from so long ago, and speaking, whispering, tempting him, telling him, to give it up, lilting and dying as his heart pounds harder, to give it up, to release his grip and give it up. Trembling with fatigue his foot slips, sending a shower of stones over the edge into the darkness where they seem suspended in a pure silence, broken after several seconds by a volley of dull explosions. It is a seductive silence, pulling him down like the cold water of the village stream, weighing heavily on his bones with its promise of a quick and lasting peace. But gradually the ridge begins to widen and he is able to walk, leaning forward, up the starlit slopes, pacing himself as best he can, breathing easily, consciously, trying to keep the voice at bay. Soon he comes to a bronze age wall built of stones as wide as several men and as he climbs it he sees from out of the west a small bright light pass quickly through the meridian constellations to drop beyond the eastern horizon, leaving him to wonder, without the hope of an answer, from where beyond the western stars it has come, where in all the vastness of night it has gone. He edges down the side of the wall to a grove of pines and seeing nothing but darkness around him, decides to lie on the damp ground and wait for morning. Shy of his scent, a genet circles at some distance and retreats. Dew falls dripping from the trees like the ticking of a living clock, peppering then pausing, as if playing out a thought. Silent as the fall of snow, the wings of a white owl beat overhead as it hangs on the air, hovering, haunting. When it moves off there is nothing for a long while, then a single bird begins to sing and swatches of sky begin to brighten among the trees. He rises just before the sun and continues upward through the pines, over the low rubble of a second wall, and on across a wet field of gravel and wild horses to the base of the dome. Several ruined huts, quarried from the third and final wall, lie under a glossy cover of ivy falling from cracks and crevices in the mass of granite whose violets and blues lighten to pinks and creams as the sun burns through the morning haze. He crawls and stumbles over the rocky heaps of the broken hovels to the smooth sides of the stone summit where he places flat the palms of his hands and presses himself as close as he can. Then he sidles along to a narrow cleft stained with moisture and moss and grasps at the roots of tenacious plants to climb, bracing with his back, pushing with his feet, pulling with his hands, until lifting himself up with a lightness newly found, through the fissure, through the shadow, to a broad flat surface of desolate stone, wind-ravaged, rain-beaten, bare floor of heaven, height of awe no longer known.

One more time for one more venture he lifts his bones to be
standing and moves them enough to be going and glad he is to
be seeing it to its end to be finishing off with such a flourish
such a palette full of summer color through fields yarrow-
trimmed like lace purfled blue-starred by gentians blooming
all around great boulders flushed an ocher pink in the sultry
light that lies like glass or golden foil on the dazzling filigree of
dancing grasses as through to the cool mixed forest and deep
fern glades he goes down through circinate fronds coyly rising
along a stream where stones themselves seem to sweat an iron
scent of metal earth and mayflies are making the most of their
day in the sun over limpid pools gathering brimful and falling
softly sounding softly rushing to gather below and fall again as
down he goes and on picking midsummer plants to pass the
time picking foxglove first the lordly foxglove and then fennel
from the nettles splendid fennel and newly fallen walnut cat-
kins and green and supple alder switches and the wild and
wrinkled yellow iris picking from here picking from there as he
goes down and on a sundry harvest of forest flowers clusters
from the elder shrub pink blossoms from the common mallow
tight russet crowns of downy mugwort when seeing far below
through a gap in the trees a village foundering it seems as if
pitched by a wave of forest against the rocky foot of the mountain glimpsed just glimpsed a moment as he goes as he wanders on lashing his bundle of plants with a hemp of bindweed
to hang from his neck to swing at his breast before starting
another before loading his arm with white bryony torn from its
corkscrew tendrils and the lithe gypsywort growing in tall green

spears and feverfew the aromatic or so they call it and leaves he plucks from the pedunculate oak and roses wild roses he rifles from a clutch of rocks and finally finally from the ground all around the male fern twice pinnate which once picked pressed and compacted he likewise lashes hangs from his neck and swings to his back as an axe swings somewhere striking solidly sounding hollowly through the forest while voices sonorous voices call calling as the stream falling drowns their fading and stonechats fly unseen to light unheard on branches higher in a place safer beyond the last echo vanishing where echoes vanish as down he goes so far down through thrips or thunder flies a cloud of tiny motes of pesky life that land on his face and hair and enter his ears before he blows them off brushes them out and passes along bound on his way down the steadfast path of paths turning at a forest junction west into a winding lane walled and floored with ancient ageless stones tunneling through the sunless bowers beneath the arches of languorous branches rising with the land falling with the land curving around the foot of the mountain past an orange and lemon orchard up a slope and into the village seen from above far above abandoned long before the tale began and the dream of breakers surging was dreamed across the salt-marsh but no dream now these crows clamoring circling above their pine colonies and the bees humming by on their homeward course looping toward small holes in the stone walls of the first house he encounters a farmhouse of fitted granite blocks and blue windows shut against the elements and stone-colored lizards frozen on the sun-baked stoop where he sits to eat an orange and gaze at the sea the misting surf beyond the trees and drowse drift and drowse as his eyelids drop his shoulders droop and his head falls heavily to one side and again until he sheds his weary sleep rises to his feet and yawning and stretching strolls back down into the shadow of pines and oaks of alders and laurels along the lane past the lasting ruins of a second house past its gutted barn of grassy beams gone to seed and on down over the trickle of hardly a stream below an empty chapel on a rock where he stops looks and finds a steep and stony climb through a yard of nettles and vetch to a house of grand estate

118

sitting close beneath the ledge of a bluff lush with ferns and hanging flowers dripping steady drops down into a pool clear and pure rising from blue subterranean sources where he pauses to drink drink his fill before turning to thread his way back through saplings of all sorts through brambles and bracken through vines weedy vines densely matted like verdant blankets breaking choking bending low the undergrowth creeping up walls crowding onto balconies to be cleared from the door before he pushes in a panel and lifts the latch and enters the gloom and dank of closed rooms the darkness and rot pierced by rays of yellow light sharpened through split shutters reaching the stairs he ascends of eastern ebony treading carefully over crumbling steps sponge soft from the festering damp to a second floor where he opens a door of frosted glass to a hall brightly lit the shutters having fallen given way to muscular trunks of ivy feeding on the old wood fanning out along the walls and ceiling and there at the end of the hall before an open window among the leaves and plaster and droppings of mice fresh as the day stands a cradle silk-lined and set rocking rocking silently by an unknown hand rocking still as he turns away and retraces his steps descends the stairs and crosses the yard to the pool where he spreads the flowers and leaves of his bundles evenly over the still surface drops his clothes on a clump of thistle and eases himself into the cold crystalline water to lie forgetful as long as he can soothed by the spicy infusion an hour or two until the sun has gone down behind the trees and he is obliged to dress without drying and hurry on through the nettles down along the lane past the last two houses of the village and into the narrow corridor of a darkening grove of pines and broom and gorse and grape vines gone wild hearing blackbirds feeding among the figs smelling rosemary and spearmint on the moist evening air as far as the edge of the forest where he finds himself before a final tract of open ground a desolate waste of sea stock and gorse and pale pine seedlings well above the inhabited plain he takes care to avoid keeping as much as he can to the rough contours and rocky soil until he crosses the coastal road and comes down through sandy fields of stunted corn and withered scarecrows salt-spray stained as black-crowned finches tumble on the sea-skimming breeze that bends the blooming spurge along the treeless lane as far down as the rounded stones above the beach where he leaves his shoes and socks to walk barefoot across the cooling sand in the rose and lemon light of cloud and sky listening to the buffet and muffled wash of cuffs of waves breaking against littoral granite combing with white fingers the clefts and kelp then flopping like an afterthought pooling streaming in sleek work of stone-wearing whispers racing sizzling up the sloping sand in broad white fans before retreating with a sigh into the gelid mass of liquid green pulling back folding rolling in upon itself before rearing again for another assault as he drags a pair of timber poles down from a stone shed to slip beneath the stern of a blue and white boat above the reach of tidal wrack and moving around to the other end he sets his shoulder to the crescent keel and pushing pushing pushes the craft down the smooth runners as far down as to touch the lilting tide lifting lightly eagerly at the buoyant stern as he gathers gathers in the anchor and climbs aboard with a firm shove to slide free of the bed of shingle and sand lying just below the hull before turning once twice with a single oar slicing hoary froth from the curling fringe of spitting waves feeling for control as up and down he goes over pitch and roll up and down and out out through a small sargasso out past the last rocks where cormorants huddle like still shadows out and on out into the open bay aligning the prow to the evening star bound as he could only be for the lilac flakes of light riding on the deep green surface of the distant sea